He opened the door in a courteous manner that made her think chivalry was alive and well in Manhattan.

She glanced over her shoulder, taking in the stunning view one more time. But not through the office window that looked out at the Empire State Building.

It was the fair-haired "cowboy" who'd caught her eye and made her heart skip a beat.

He slid her a smile. "I'll call you."

She knew he was talking about the case. But somewhere, deep in her heart, she wondered what it would be like to wait for another kind of call from him.

A personal call.

Still, that was silly. The man probably had a legion of women clamoring for his attention.

And Priscilla wasn't planning to ride off into the sunset with anyone....

Dear Reader,

No matter what the weather is like, I always feel like March 1st is the beginning of spring. So let's celebrate that just-around-the-corner thaw with, for starters, another of Christine Rimmer's beloved BRAVO FAMILY TIES books. In *The Bravo Family Way,* a secretive Las Vegas mogul decides he "wants" a beautiful preschool owner who's long left the glittering lights and late nights of Vegas behind. But she hadn't counted on the charms of Fletcher Bravo. No woman could resist him for long....

Victoria Pade's *The Baby Deal,* next up in our FAMILY BUSINESS continuity, features wayward son Jack Hanson finally agreeing to take a meeting with a client—only perhaps he got a little too friendly too fast? She's pregnant, and he's...well, he's not sure what he is, quite frankly. In Judy Duarte's *Call Me Cowboy,* a New York City girl is in desperate need of a detective with a working knowledge of Texas to locate the mother she's never known. Will she find everything she's looking for, courtesy of T. J. "Cowboy" Whittaker? In *She's the One,* Patricia Kay's conclusion to her CALLIE'S CORNER CAFÉ series, a woman who's always put her troublesome younger sister's needs before her own finds herself torn by her attraction to the handsome cop who's about to place said sister under arrest. Lois Faye Dyer's new miniseries, THE McCLOUDS OF MONTANA, which features two feuding families, opens with *Luke's Proposal.* In it, the daughter of one family is forced to work together with the son of the other—with very unexpected results! And in *A Bachelor at the Wedding* by Kate Little, a sophisticated Manhattan tycoon finds himself relying more and more on his Brooklyn-bred assistant (yeah, Brooklyn)—and not just for business.

So enjoy, and come back next month—the undisputed start of spring....

Gail

Please address questions and book requests to:
Silhouette Reader Service
U.S.: 3010 Walden Ave., P.O. Box 1325, Buffalo, NY 14269
Canadian: P.O. Box 609, Fort Erie, Ont. L2A 5X3

CALL ME COWBOY

JUDY DUARTE

Silhouette

SPECIAL EDITION®

Published by Silhouette Books

America's Publisher of Contemporary Romance

To my favorite associates at WalMart #2094 in Vista, California:

Valeen Archibald, Lydia Bustos, Donna Camper, Sarah Colwell,
Bobbie Hernandez, Judy Pace, Mary Murphy and Norma Rubio.

Thanks for your support!

And a special thank-you to Nevalyn Annese, the Anderson sales rep
who made my book signing such a great experience.

You girls rock!

SILHOUETTE BOOKS

ISBN 0-373-24743-5

CALL ME COWBOY

Copyright © 2006 by Judy Duarte

Visit Silhouette Books at www.eHarlequin.com

Printed in U.S.A.

JUDY DUARTE

An avid reader who enjoys a happy ending, Judy Duarte loves to create stories of her own. When she's not cooped up in her writing cave, she's spending time with her somewhat enormous, but delightfully close family.

Judy makes her home in California with her personal hero, their youngest son and a cat named Mom. "Sharing a name with the family pet gets a bit confusing," she admits. "Especially when the cat decides to curl up in a secluded cubbyhole and hide. I'm not sure what the neighbors think when my son walks up and down the street calling for Mom."

You can write to Judy c/o Silhouette Books, 233 Broadway, Suite 1001, New York, NY 10237. Or you can contact her through her Web site at: www.judyduarte.com.

Dear Reader,

I hope you enjoy reading *Call Me Cowboy* as much as I did writing it.

In fact, as part of the fun, I'll be sponsoring a special contest on my Web site during the month of March 2006.

What kind of contest?

Why a chili cook-off, of course!

If you think your favorite recipe can compete with Becky Epperson's Snake-adillo Chili, enter online at: www.JudyDuarte.com. But since this is a cybercontest, your secret recipe will remain safe and yours alone. All you have to do is enter the *name* of your special chili.

The winner will be announced on my Web site on April 15, 2006, and will receive a six-month subscription to the Special Edition book club and have a choice of five autographed books from my backlist. There will be prizes for the runners-up, too.

So why not fire up your computer and head over to my Web site now? See you there!

Wishing you romance and a happy-ever-after.

Judy Duarte

Prologue

Cotton Creek, Texas

The stairway creaked, and Priscilla opened her eyes. It was dark, and someone big was carrying her.

"Daddy?"

"Shhh, baby girl. It's okay. I have you."

Only the Snoopy night-light lit their way.

"Where are we going?"

He shushed her. "Go back to sleep, honey."

Priscilla rested her head on her daddy's chest, nuzzling her cheek against the soft flannel of his shirt, feeling the steady beat of his heart, the familiar buckle in his step as he limped toward the front door.

She yawned. "I'm really tired, Daddy."

"I know, baby."

Priscilla didn't want to get up. She wanted to go back to her bed, with its Pound Puppies sheets and bedspread.

As they stepped outside and Daddy carefully closed the front door, the night air cooled her face and her bare toes.

A hoot owl called from the trees, and a doggy barked in someone else's yard.

"It's cold, Daddy. And it's dark."

"Everything is going to be just fine, honey. You wait and see." Daddy carried her for a while, down the driveway and to the street, where he'd parked his truck.

The engine was running, and the heater made it all warm and cozy.

"I have a pillow and blanket for you," he told her. "Why don't you try and go back to sleep. We have a long drive ahead."

"Where are we going?" she asked as she crawled across the seat.

"To a happy place," he told her as he climbed into the pickup and closed the door.

Priscilla looked over her shoulder and out the back window. She could hardly see the house, until a light went on in the upstairs window.

"Where's Mama?" she asked. "Why isn't she going with us?"

"Go back to sleep, honey. We'll call her in the morning and you can talk to her."

They drove all that night and the next day, but they never did stop and call Mama.

And they didn't talk about her anymore either.

Chapter One

Twenty-two years later

Priscilla Richards wasn't in the party spirit, but she held a full glass of champagne and went through the social motions—the feigned smiles, the required chitchat.

Outside, the night was bright and clear. Inside, the penthouse was elegant, the decor festive.

Byron Van Zandt, an investment banker, had spared no expense in throwing a first-class celebration for his daughter Sylvia's recent promotion. He'd even hired a violinist through the philharmonic. So it wasn't any wonder that the mood of those in attendance was upbeat.

Well, not everyone's.

Priscilla was ready to thank her host and go home.

But not because she wasn't happy for the young woman of honor.

She and Sylvia had met at Brown University, where they'd both graduated with a master's degree in literary arts. Then they'd landed dream jobs at Sunshine Valley Books, a small but growing publisher that specialized in children's literature.

Being colleagues had only deepened their friendship, so there was no way Priscilla would have made an excuse to stay home, where she'd prefer to be.

She just wished she could be more enthusiastic for her best friend's sake.

"Hey," Sylvia said, making her way to Priscilla's side with a half-filled flute of champagne. "You're *finally* here!"

"I wouldn't miss it." Priscilla managed a weak but sincere smile. "Congratulations on the promotion."

Sylvia, with her dark hair cropped in a short but stylish cut, nodded toward Priscilla's full glass. "I hope that's not your first."

It was, so she nodded.

"Drink up, Pris. You can crash here. No need to worry about going back to Brooklyn tonight."

"Thanks for the offer, but I need to get home. In fact, I'm going to cut out early."

Sylvia drew closer and studied Priscilla intently. "You know, I'm starting to worry about you."

"I'll be okay. Really."

Apparently Sylvia wasn't convinced, because she crossed her arms and shifted her weight to one leg. "I know you adored your father, Pris. And it's normal to grieve. But I hate to see you so down. Maybe you ought to talk to a doctor and get some medication. Or better yet, why don't you make an appointment with a professional, like a minister or a counselor?"

It wasn't grief that had knocked her for a loop.

Priscilla placed an arm around Sylvia and gave her an affectionate squeeze. "Thanks for the advice. But all I really need to do is bite the bullet and go through my dad's belongings. I'll be fine after that."

"Does that mean you'll be returning to work soon? Ever since you took that leave of absence, I haven't had anyone to gossip with. And right now I think the new receptionist is sleeping with Larry in Marketing."

"Syl, you never gossip."

"Only with you." Sylvia took a sip of champagne. "So when are you coming back to work?"

Up until last night, Priscilla had planned to go into the office on Monday morning.

Now she wasn't so sure. "I may need to request another week or so."

Sylvia clucked her tongue. "Aw, Pris. Come stay with me for a while. You've been cooped up in that brownstone for months and need a change of scenery. We can make fudge and eat ice cream, which always makes *me* feel better. And we'll pull out my entire collection of Hugh Grant DVDs."

"Thanks, Syl. Let me take care of a few things and I'll take you up on it. But no more Hugh Grant movies."

"How about Mel Gibson?"

"Only if he's wearing a white cowboy hat and boots. I'm leaning toward the John Wayne type." Someone who *didn't* remind her of her father.

"Mmm. Mel in a cowboy hat. I'll see what I can do." Sylvia chuckled, then changed to a serious tone. "Can't you wait and go through your dad's belongings in a couple of weeks?"

"No, I'm afraid not." Priscilla's curiosity was fast becoming a compulsion to find answers to the questions she'd had. Questions she'd been afraid to voice.

"Well," Sylvia said, "it must be a relief to know your father isn't suffering anymore."

The last few months, as cancer had racked his body, Priscilla had taken time off work to care for him. It had been a drain to see him waste away, to know how much pain he'd suffered.

"You're right, Syl. He's in a better place."

"And there's another upside," her friend added. "He's with your mom now."

Priscilla nodded. It hadn't been any big secret that Clinton Richards had been devastated after losing his wife more than twenty years ago. And rather than look for another woman to love, he'd devoted his life to his daughter, to her happiness and well-being. In fact, when Priscilla had been accepted to Brown University, he'd moved to Providence, Rhode Island, just to be close to her. And when she'd landed the job with Sunshine Valley Books, he'd relocated again—to New York. Fortunately, as a self-employed Web site designer, he worked out of the home and had a flexibility other fathers didn't have.

Priscilla hooked her arm through Sylvia's and drew her toward the front door. "Listen, Syl. This has been a great party, but I really need to get home."

"Oh, no you don't." Her friend lifted a nearly empty champagne flute. "You need to finish that drink and mingle."

"Actually my stomach has been bothering me the past couple of days." Okay, maybe not for days, but ever since last night, when that unsettling dream woke her at two in the morning. And it had intensified when she'd padded into her father's bedroom and begun to dig through his cedar chest.

"I'll bet it's the stress you've been under that's affecting your stomach," Sylvia said.

"Probably." But it was more than grief bothering her. She just wished she could put her finger on exactly what had knocked her digestive system out of whack.

She did, however, have a clue.

The mild-mannered widower who'd loved her had taken a secret to his grave. A secret Priscilla was determined to uncover.

Would she feel better if she confided in Sylvia?

Maybe, although now didn't seem to be the time.

On the other hand, keeping Sylvia worried and in

the dark might put a damper on an evening when she ought to be celebrating.

Priscilla took a long, deep breath, then slowly let it out. "I had a dream last night and woke up in tangled sheets and a cold sweat."

"A nightmare?" Sylvia asked. "Those can be pretty upsetting."

"Yes, they can. But so can a repressed memory, which is what I think it was."

Sylvia stopped a waiter walking by, placed her flute on his tray and gave Priscilla her undivided attention. "What do you mean?"

She wasn't sure. At first, it had been a niggling, restless feeling. Then there'd been a collage of images.

A two-story house. The scent of vanilla and spice. Laughter. Bedtime stories.

Loud voices and tears.

A marble-topped table crashing to the floor.

The remnants of her dream, of the memory, of her odd discovery, settled over her like a cold, wet blanket.

She tried her best to shake it off, at least long enough to level with her friend. "When I woke up, I felt so uneasy that I went into my father's room and opened the old chest where he kept his things and went through it."

"What did you find?"

"Evidence that my name might not be Priscilla Richards."

"Wow." Sylvia furrowed her brow, then cocked her head in disbelief. "Are you sure?"

"No. I'm not. But until I get to the bottom of this, I won't be able to focus on anything else. I just wish I knew where to start digging."

Sylvia stood silent, focused. Then she brightened. "Wait here."

"Where are you going?"

Without answering, Sylvia dashed off, swerving to avoid a waitress balancing a tray of hors d'oeuvres, and ducked into her father's study.

Oh, for Pete's sake. Sylvia could be so dramatic. But like a child waiting for guidance, Priscilla remained in the entryway.

Moments later Sylvia returned and placed a glossy business card in Priscilla's hand. "This is the firm my dad uses for employee screenings."

Priscilla scanned the card.

> Garcia and Associates
> Elite and Discreet Investigations
> Offices in Chicago, Los Angeles and Manhattan
> Trenton J. Whittaker

"The agency is reputable and well respected," Sylvia said. "Of course, they're not cheap. But I'd be happy to loan you whatever you need."

"Thanks. But my dad had a healthy savings account he transferred to me before he died. And he also had a good-sized life insurance policy. So I'll be all right."

"For what it's worth," Sylvia added, eyes growing bright and a grin busting out on her face, "I met that guy—Trenton Whittaker—at my dad's office the other day. And he's to die for. You ought to hear the soft Southern drawl of his voice. It's so darn sexy it'll make you melt in a puddle on the floor."

Priscilla rolled her eyes. "When I choose a private investigator, it won't be based upon his looks or the sound of his voice."

"You can't go wrong with Garcia and Associates. They're a top-of-the-line agency. And if the P.I. also happens to be single and hot, what's the problem? Heaven knows your love life could sure use a shot in the tush. And believe me, Pris, this guy will do it. If I weren't involved with Warren, I'd have jumped his bones in a heartbeat."

Priscilla wasn't interested in finding Mr. Right. After all, she couldn't very well expect a happily ever after when she'd had too many questions about once upon a time.

But she took the card and slid it into her purse, figuring she'd give the agency—not necessarily Mr. Whittaker—a try.

Then she handed Sylvia her nearly full glass of champagne. "Congratulations on the promotion. Thanks for inviting me."

"Don't thank me for that." Sylvia placed the glass on a table in the entry. "You're my best friend."

"And you're mine." Priscilla gave her a hug.

"Hey. I just thought of something."

Priscilla waited, poised by the door. "What's that?"

"Remember that young-adult book you edited a while back? The one about the rodeo cowboy?"

It had been well written, the settings vivid, the character a handsome young man with true grit and brawn.

Priscilla nodded. "What about it?"

"You told me that you could see yourself riding off into the sunset with a cowboy like that."

"So? I didn't mean anything by it." And she hadn't. It had just been a dreamy, romantic comment. After all, Priscilla loved the Big Apple and thrived in a cosmopolitan environment. She even found the hustle and bustle thrilling. So for that reason alone, when it came to a lover, a cowboy was out of the question.

"I saw the way your eyes lit up, the way you placed your hand on the cover of that book. You practically caressed the cowboy on the front. That was your heart speaking, Pris. And have I found the perfect man for you."

"What are you talking about? A man is the last thing in the world I need right now."

"How about a Manhattan-based P.I. with a slow Southern drawl? A man they call Cowboy."

"Cowboy" Whittaker sat behind his desk in the Manhattan office of Garcia and Associates with his back to an impressive view of the Empire State Building.

He'd just gotten off the phone with a client, an appreciative single mother who'd called to tell him she'd received her first child-support check. And thanks to the work Cowboy had done in locating her ex—a man who'd run off with an off-Broadway showgirl—the runaway daddy's wages were now being garnished, and he was being forced to support the kids he'd fathered.

Deadbeat dads were the worst.

Not that Cowboy was an expert on fathers. His had been a workaholic who'd never had time for his family. But at least there'd been plenty of money to go around.

He blew out a sigh. He was eager to get back in the field, to do what he did best—charming the secrets out of unwitting folks with his down-home, slow and easy style.

Cowboy's Southern twang often gave people the impression that he was a backwoods hick—which couldn't be any further from the truth—and they tended to open up with him, sharing things they wouldn't share with another investigator. So he used it to his advantage, sometimes even laying it on extra thick.

God, he loved his job, the mind games that uncovered secrets and revealed lies.

What he didn't love was working indoors, confined to an office.

But until his boss and buddy, Rico Garcia, returned from his honeymoon in Tahiti, Cowboy was deskbound.

Fortunately Rico was due back in town tomorrow evening.

As Cowboy scanned a report sent in by an associate, the intercom buzzed.

Margie, the office manager, was probably telling him his three o'clock appointment had arrived—a referral from Byron Van Zandt, one of their newer clients.

He clicked on the flashing button. "Yes, ma'am."

"Priscilla Richards is here, Cowboy."

"Thank you. Will you please send her in?" He closed the file he'd been reading and slid it across the polished desk.

As the door swung open, he stood to greet the woman—one of many formalities and courtesies his mother had instilled in him while he'd been growing up in the upper echelon of Dallas society.

Margie opened the door and stepped aside as an attractive redhead dressed in a conservative cream-colored skirt and jacket entered the office. She stood about five-three or -four. A pretty tumble of red hair had been swept into a neat, professional twist.

She wore only a whisper of lipstick and a dab of mascara. She didn't need any more makeup than that.

Some women looked like a million bucks when they went out on the town in the evenings, but woke up as scary as hell. Yet he suspected this one looked damn good in the morning even before she climbed out of bed.

A man might be tempted to find out for himself if that were true or not—if he were attracted to the prim, classy type.

But Cowboy had been turned off by that kind ever since his mother had begun prying into his dating habits as a teenager and tried to set him up with one Dallas debutante after another. It might have started as a good case of adolescent rebellion, but he'd been drawn to fun-lovin' gals who knew how to party ever since.

But that was when he was off duty. He didn't date his clients, although he'd been known to flirt some— just to make life interesting.

Still, he found himself intrigued by this prim little package, curious about her story.

Maybe it was the red curls that seemed to beg to break free of confinement, hinting that she knew how to let her hair down and kick up her heels. Or those big blue eyes that could snare a fellow and drag him into something too close for comfort.

But the white-knuckle way she held the shoulder strap of her purse suggested she might hightail it out of his office at any time.

Dang. He always liked to see shy women loosen up, relax, feel comfortable around him—even if that was as far as things went.

He moved to the front of his desk and touched the back of the leather chair reserved for clients and providing them with a twenty-third-floor view of the city. "Why don't you have a seat, ma'am?"

"Thank you, Mr. Whittaker."

He flashed her a charming smile meant to disarm her. "No need to call me Mr. I go by TJ at home in

Dallas and Cowboy here in Manhattan. You can take your pick."

She cleared her throat, obviously a little nervous, which kicked up his curiosity another notch.

He sat, the leather of his desk chair creaking beneath his weight. "What can I do for you?"

"I'm not sure where to begin. This is all so new to me." Her voice, a soft, sexy purr like the other side of a pay-for-sex telephone conversation, slid over him like a silk scarf across bare skin.

Not that he made those calls—other than that night he and Dave Hamilton had gotten drunk when they were in the tenth grade.

Is that why she wrapped herself in a nine-to-five business suit? To mask the sexual aura of a voice that could earn a fortune working for 1-900-Dial-A-Hard-On?

Enough of that. He roped in his thoughts and tried to keep his mind on work. "Why don't you start at the beginning?"

She leaned back in her seat, yet her demeanor remained stiff, her hands poised on her lap. "A couple of days ago I had an unsettling dream." She took a breath, then slowly let it out. "But it was *so* real. It had to be a dormant memory."

Some dreams could seem real when they weren't, but he let her talk.

"It woke me at two in the morning. My heart was pounding and I had this uneasy feeling."

"What did you dream about?" he asked.

"When I was only three or so, my daddy carried me to his pickup in the middle of the night, then drove straight through to the small town in Iowa where I grew up."

"A lot of folks start a long trip before sunrise," he said. "It's easier to drive when the roads are clear of traffic."

"Yes, but my father kept shushing me as we walked down the stairs and out the front door. He told me that everything would be all right."

"Is that what you remember? Or was that part of the dream?"

"It was too real to ignore, so I went into my father's bedroom and began sorting through his things, something I'd been putting off."

Cowboy assumed she must have found something that validated her suspicion. A gut feeling wasn't much to go on. And he wouldn't take her money if he suspected the investigation would only be a crap-shoot. He needed more information than what she'd already given him.

"My dad had this old cedar chest that he'd made in a high school shop class. And he stored his things in it, like an Army uniform, a Boy Scout shirt with all his badges." She looked at him with glistening blue eyes. "He was an Eagle Scout."

Was she thinking that precluded her old man from lying or keeping something a secret?

"His Army dispatch papers were in there, too," she added.

"And?"

"My father's real name was apparently Clifford Richard Epperson, not Clinton Richards. And I need someone to help me uncover the reason why he changed his name."

"Is that all?" he asked.

Yes. No. Priscilla wasn't sure.

She cleared her throat. "Well, there is one other thing, although it might not amount to anything at all."

As he waited for her come up with a response, Mr. Whittaker—or rather, Cowboy—leaned back in his chair. She found it impossible not to study him, not to be intrigued by him.

He was a big man. Tall. Well over six feet when he stood. His light brown hair appeared stylishly mussed, but she suspected that was due to the white cowboy hat resting on the other side of the huge mahogany desk at which he sat. His hazel eyes glistened like amber in the sunlight. And his voice was enough to lull a woman into mindless submission.

Sylvia had been right about his soft Southern drawl.

It's so darn sexy it'll make you melt in a puddle on the floor.

"What's that?" he asked.

"Excuse me?" Her cheeks warmed as she realized he'd been waiting for her to answer while she'd been gawking and pondering things best left alone.

"You mentioned there was one other thing I ought to know."

"Oh, yes. I was so wrapped up in…uh…the memory and trying to sort through it." She cleared her throat again, hoping to dislodge the lame excuse for the sexual direction in which her thoughts had drifted.

"Then take your time." He rocked in his seat, the leather chair creaking from his weight. But she focused on the task at hand, on the information she ought to share.

"My father died of cancer. And the end was pretty rough, even with hospice to help us." She tried hard to remember exactly what had been said. "Right before he slipped into a coma, I sat by his bedside and told him how much I loved him, how happy I was that he'd been both mother and father to me. That I was the luckiest daughter in the world. And that if God was calling him home, I was ready to let him go so he could join my mother."

Cowboy didn't comment, so she continued.

"My dad gripped my hand, then tried to speak. He said something about my mother, but the words were garbled. I did pick up an 'I'm sorry.' And a bit later, 'God forgive me.' I assumed he meant he was sorry for dying and leaving me alone. That he was trying to make peace with God so that he could go to heaven."

"And now you're not so sure?"

No. A memory seemed to be just under the surface, waiting to be revealed.

"I'm not sure what to think. But I want to know why he changed his name. That would be a good start." She reached into her purse and pulled out a yellowed envelope. It held her father's discharge papers, along with her birth certificate, which listed Clinton and Jezzie Richards as her parents. "You see? His names don't match."

"When did your father die?"

"The Fourth of July. Independence Day." She smiled wryly. "It's kind of ironic, I suppose. He'd never wanted me to be alone."

Cowboy glanced down at the paperwork. "It shouldn't be too difficult to trace his steps."

"Good. It's time for me to go back to work, to put my life back on track. But I can't face the future without knowing what happened in the past." And until she got some answers it would be impossible for her to focus on the stories she edited, the tales meant to provide children with warm fuzzies. Not when her own childhood was so unsettling.

And confusing.

While in college, she'd categorized her memories into levels, like the stories she now edited.

The time she and her father had lived in Iowa had been the chapter-book years, and the memories were abundant and happy.

But she had very little recollection of the picture-book years, just the flash of an image, the sound of a soft but undistinguishable voice.

A big white house with a step that squeaked—the one at the bottom of the landing. A Snoopy night-light with a broken ear. A tire swing under an old oak tree.

A faceless dark-haired woman who made sugar cookies with little colored sprinkles on top.

"Where can I reach you?" Cowboy asked.

She slipped her hand into her purse for a business card, then pulled out a pen and jotted down her home and cell phone numbers. Then she handed it to him.

He glanced at the card that displayed a colorful child's sketch of a sun in the top left-hand corner and a small tree at the bottom right.

"Sunshine Valley Books," he read out loud. "Priscilla Richards, Associate Editor."

"We publish children's literature," she said.

He chuckled, his hazel eyes glimmering with mirth. "I was close."

"Close?" she asked. "I don't understand."

"I had you pegged as the librarian type."

She smiled. Sylvia had probably pegged him right, too. Cowboy Whittaker was a charmer. And she suspected he was a footloose bachelor who'd never met a woman he didn't want to wine or dine.

Or bed.

Not that Priscilla was interested in being another in a long line of conquests.

But that didn't mean she didn't appreciate his style. Or his looks.

"You know," she said as she stood and slipped the strap of her purse over her shoulder, "I really like the sound of your voice. Your accent is…" She paused, unable to finish her line of thought. She couldn't very well tell him that she found it sexy. So she reached for something more appropriate. "Your voice is gentle on the ears."

"Well, now. Ain't that something. I'm pretty partial to the sound of your voice, too." He tossed her a boyish grin. "It's as sexy as all get out."

She swallowed, unsure of what to say.

Was he flirting with her?

Or teasing?

Either way, she dropped the thought like the wrong end of a hot curling iron.

He followed her to the door, then reached for the knob. "I assume Margie has already gone over our rates."

Priscilla nodded. "Yes, she has. And I gave her a deposit."

"It shouldn't take more than a couple of days to get some kind of answer for you. And we can take it from there."

She nodded. "Thanks. I appreciate this."

He opened the door in a courteous manner that made her think that chivalry was alive and well in Manhattan.

As she stepped out of his office, she glanced over her shoulder, taking in the stunning view one more time.

But not through the office window that looked out at the Empire State Building.

It was the fair-haired "cowboy" who'd caught her eye and made her heart skip a beat.

He slid her a smile. "I'll call you."

She knew he was talking about the case. But somewhere deep in her heart she wondered what it would be like to wait for another kind of call from him.

A personal call.

But that was silly. The man probably had a legion of women clamoring for his attention. And Priscilla wasn't planning to ride off into the sunset with anyone.

Not until she'd come to grips with her past and uncovered her father's secret.

Chapter Two

As the sun hovered over Manhattan, Cowboy turned his desk chair a hundred and eighty degrees, providing him with a view of the city.

His day was growing crappier by the minute.

First his mother had called, insisting he come home in a couple of weeks for a fancy dinner party she was having, a formal wingding to kick off his brother-in-law's campaign for congressman.

It was a command performance for all the Whittakers, he supposed. But it was an event the family black sheep wasn't eager to attend.

The youngest son of an oil-rich family, Trenton James Whittaker had been born a maverick. And his prim and proper mother had been hell-bent on taming him since day one. But Cowboy—or rather, TJ to folks in Dallas—had never been the submissive sort.

His mother had finally given up trying to control him. But that hadn't stopped her from doing her damnedest to set him up with every "suitable" debutante or socialite she could find, hoping the right woman would make him toe the mark.

TJ hadn't been interested in any of them and he'd responded to her meddling by bringing home "dates" he knew she'd never approve of.

Not that he'd set up an unsuspecting woman for an inquisition or a snub. His "dates" had all been friends or acquaintances who'd known what they were getting into. And they'd dressed for the occasion.

It was part of the game.

Elena Cruz, the last gal he'd taken home, had walked into the Whittaker estate sporting stilettos, a black miniskirt and a bare midriff revealing a belly-button ring and a stick-on tattoo.

Later, over a beer, he and Elena had laughed about his mother's reaction.

But there was a hell of a lot more going on between him and his mom than rebellion.

For the past fifteen years they'd been involved in a cold war, an undeclared conflict that had started when she'd walked into the living room unexpectedly and found him and Jenny Dugan sharing a tongue-swapping kiss. She'd embarrassed the poor girl so badly that, as far as TJ was concerned, she'd triggered a set of circumstances that had led to Jenny's death. And he'd never really forgiven his mom for that.

Not that she'd asked him to.

Maybe that's why he'd continued to be a burr under her saddle, a thorn in her side.

He hadn't been as contrary or ornery lately, though. But that's because he'd grown tired of the family rigmarole and gone to New York on a whim, a visit that had become permanent after he'd met Rico and landed a job with Garcia and Associates.

Absence might not have made his heart grow fonder, but his life had become a hell of a lot more peaceful.

He glanced at the calendar. July twenty-third was wide open, so he'd fly to Dallas that weekend and attend the dinner party—for his sister's sake.

While on the telephone, he'd told his mother as much.

Still, it had been more than his mother's call that had sent his day on a downhill slide.

He'd just uncovered information that would set his latest client's world on end. And he wasn't looking forward to telling her.

His first impulse had been to call Priscilla Richards so that he wouldn't have to deal with her tears and emotion in person. But that would be the coward's way out. A face-to-face meeting was definitely in order—even if he wasn't up for it.

"Hey," a familiar voice sounded from the open doorway to the lobby.

Cowboy turned and shot Rico an ain't-you-a-sight-for-sore-eyes grin.

He didn't have to ask how the honeymoon trip to Tahiti had been. Rico wore a sugar-pie-honey-bunch smile that claimed he was bonkers in love and content to be hog-tied to one woman for the rest of his life.

Cowboy chuckled. "It's about time you got back here, lover boy."

"I thought I'd better make sure my right-hand man hadn't run the company into the ground while I was away." Rico made his way across the office toward Cowboy's desk. "How's it going?"

"So far so good."

Rico studied him for a moment. "You're not one to ponder the city view, no matter now nice it is. What's the matter?"

"Just another invitation from home due to social protocol and an effort to keep up pretenses." Cowboy shrugged. "But I've also got to break some bad news to a client and I'm not looking forward to it."

"Anyone I know?"

"No, she's brand-new. A referral from Byron Van Zandt."

"*She?*" Rico asked. "That should make it easy. You're an ace at handling ladies and turning on the charm."

Cowboy chuffed. "Not this time."

"Why not?"

"She's not the kind of woman I charm. That's all."

Priscilla might not have the wealth and social standing of some of Dallas's haute single crowd, but she was one of them just the same. The kind of woman who cared about her reputation and had serious expectations of the men she dated, men she could control and force to go to all those high-society functions. And he'd be damned if he'd let one of them try to hog-tie him and drag him off to honeymoon heaven.

Rico plopped down in the chair in front of Cowboy's desk. "Sounds like she's either an old biddy or a gal just like the one that married dear ole Dad. Which is it?"

Cowboy cracked a wry smile. "She's not old. And if she'd shed that prim and proper shell, she'd be a real looker. But my gut tells me she's too damn nice for the likes of me. And I'm not into nice girls, remember?"

"Yeah, I do. If she had a wild streak, you'd be in a real pickle, especially since you don't date clients, either."

"You're right about that." Cowboy wasn't sure how this particular client had tapped into the well of sympathy that rested under his surface. But nevertheless, when he'd learned what she was up against, he'd been worried about how she'd take the news.

"So what's bothering you about the case?" Rico asked.

"I don't know. I just have this feeling she's going

to buckle and fall apart and I don't want to feel as though I should help pick up the pieces. I'm not good at that sort of thing."

Rico reached into the candy dish Cowboy kept on the desk and scooped out a handful of M&M's with peanuts. "What makes you think she'll get emotional?"

"She just lost her father, a man she loved. And I have to be the one to tell her he was a bastard in disguise."

Cowboy knew his report would open a can of emotional worms for Priscilla. And he wasn't up for the backlash—unless she surprised him and just got good and angry. He'd much rather be faced with kicking and screaming than tears.

Rico leaned back in his chair, leather and springs creaking under his weight. "What'd you find out about her old man?"

"There were a couple of outstanding warrants out for his arrest in Texas."

"What were the charges?"

"One was for assault. And the other was for kidnapping."

Priscilla sat on the floor in the middle of her father's bedroom, placing his old clothing into a box for the Salvation Army.

The room still bore his scent—a combination of Old Spice and pipe tobacco—yet a faint medicinal smell remained, reminding her of the pain he'd suffered during his final days.

It hurt to part with the things he'd once worn, but it was silly to keep his old shirts, pants and shoes when someone else could get some use out of them.

She'd already gone through the file cabinets, finding old tax returns, paid bills and the pink slip to the Ford Taurus he'd purchased nearly seven years ago. Among his things she'd discovered her birth certificate, which she'd given Cowboy. She'd also found her immunization record and old report cards.

But there was no marriage license.

Nothing from the picture-book years.

But that was to be expected. A fire caused by faulty wiring had claimed the life of her mother and burned the hundred-year-old house they'd once lived in to the ground. Everything the family had owned, including photographs and memorabilia, had been destroyed.

The only thing left was the old cedar trunk her father had made in a high-school shop class. He'd brought it to Iowa in the back of his pickup that cold, dark night when he and Priscilla had left Texas.

She placed her hand on the polished cedar. Her father had once labored over the wood, sanding it and adding lacquer to make it shine. Then he'd given it to her mother to use as a hope chest.

But instead of hopes for the future, the trunk held faded memories now.

She lifted the lid and pulled out his musty green Army uniform.

Years ago, when she'd been in middle school,

she'd walked in on him while he'd knelt before the chest, going through the contents. She'd startled him, and he'd jerked back as though she'd caught him doing something wrong.

His eyes had been red, watery, and he'd quickly balled up the shirt, tossed it back inside and closed the lid. For a moment she'd thought he was going to snap at her. Instead he'd held his tongue, brushed his hands under his eyes to remove evidence of his sadness and cleared his throat.

"How about an ice cream cone?" he'd asked.

His response had been surreal and his question had taken her aback. At the time she'd wanted to quiz him about the past, to talk to him about his grief, to share her own disappointment at having to grow up without a mother. And she'd wanted to ask some of the questions she'd been storing for years.

But whenever she'd mentioned her mother, Texas or the past, a veil of sadness had washed over his face. She'd easily concluded that there was something tender inside him, something that had never healed. A vulnerability that embarrassed him.

So, as she'd done so many times in the past, she'd tried to make it easy on him and his battered heart by leaving the past alone.

Instead she'd agreed to go for an ice cream cone, trading a double dip of rocky road for the conversation and shared tears she would have preferred.

Now, weeks after her father's death, she still knew very little about the man he'd really been.

As she studied the front of his Army shirt, she saw the scraggly loose threads where a name tag used to be.

Had he tried to hide his identity from her?

And if so, why hadn't he just ditched the uniform? Storing it made no sense.

She placed it aside and removed the Boy Scout shirt that boasted a green sash filled with badges. Archery. Swimming. Camping. Canoeing. First Aid.

It seemed as though he was holding on to the memory of his achievements. But if so, why had he kept them hidden in a trunk, hidden from her?

She removed the other items—a well-used baseball mitt, a football autographed by teammates, a Swiss Army knife, a book on hunting and camping. Apparently her father had been athletic in his youth, interested in sports and the outdoors.

Yet the man she'd known had been quiet-spoken, a bookworm. A homebody. And his only activity had been a daily walk to get the newspaper.

She'd assumed it was because of his bad leg, an old Army injury. But come to think of it, he'd never watched sports on TV or given her any indication he'd ever had an interest in anything other than her, his books and his computer.

It didn't jibe.

Who was her father?

And more importantly, who was his daughter?

Until she had the answers, Priscilla wouldn't rest.

After emptying the chest, she peered at a piece of

pink floral wallpaper that covered the bottom. One corner was curled up.

As she reached to straighten the paper lining, her fingers brushed against something underneath.

The edge of a card?

She tugged at the corner, removed the lining and spotted an old Polaroid photograph of her father wearing his Army uniform—with EPPERSON clearly printed on the name tag. He stood beside a short, dark-haired teenage girl with a pretty smile.

Was that her mother?

Priscilla couldn't recall any specific details of her mother's face, but she remembered her as a big woman, heavyset. In fact, Priscilla hadn't been able to wrap her little arms around her waist for a hug.

But the girl in the picture was slight, petite.

Priscilla studied the couple again, wishing her father were still here to talk to.

She flipped over the snapshot.

No names. No notation.

Before she could peruse the picture any longer, the doorbell rang.

It was probably Mrs. Hendrix with another casserole. The elderly widow dealt with loneliness by reaching out to people in need. And she'd been a real blessing to Priscilla these past few months, first as her father's health had deteriorated, then during the funeral arrangements and now with thoughtful gestures and visits.

Priscilla stood, brushed her hands on the fabric of

her black slacks, then padded to the living room in her bare feet.

A strand of hair had escaped the ponytail she wore, and she tucked it behind her ear. When she reached the door, she tiptoed and peered through the peephole, preparing to greet her neighbor.

But it wasn't Mavis Hendrix on the stoop; it was Mr. Whittaker—or rather, the man they called Cowboy.

Her heart thumped, then raced as she swung open the door.

He removed his hat and shot her a heart-spinning grin that warmed her cheeks.

She tried to hide her surprise and returned his smile. "Hi."

"I was in the neighborhood and thought I'd stop by to talk to you."

"I…uh…" She nodded toward the bedrooms. "I was just going through my father's things."

"Is this a bad time?"

To talk about the investigation she'd hired him to do? On the contrary, it was probably a good time. She was knee-deep in the past—or at least what little she knew about it. "No, please come in."

As the big man stepped into the living room, the walls seemed to close in on them. His cologne, something light and musky, settled around her, and she found herself savoring each whiff of his scent.

He wore faded jeans, a chambray shirt and a brown leather jacket. As he removed his hat, looking as though he'd just walked out onto a Dodge City street, she couldn't help fussing with the side of her hair and wondering if any other strands had come loose.

Her attention returned to her guest, and she watched as he scanned the room. His gaze first lit on the boxes she'd filled for the Salvation Army and then on the curtains she'd forgotten to open this morning.

"I probably should have called first," he said.

"That's all right. I've been sticking close to home these past few months." She pulled the rubber band from her hair and combed her fingers through the curly strands, hoping she hadn't made her appearance look worse. She didn't like having people see her unkempt, especially this particular someone.

When he caught her gaze, her fingers stilled and she dropped her hands to her sides. "Have you learned anything about my father?"

"Yep," he said, nodding but not smiling. "There's more investigating that needs to be done, but it's your call whether you want me to do it or whether you'd like to take the ball from here."

"I guess that depends on what you've learned."

He made his way toward her, then placed a hand on her shoulder, sending a flutter of heat through her bloodstream. "Let's take a walk."

A walk? "You don't want to talk here?"

He scanned the room again, then slowly shook his head. "Nope. I'm a fresh-air-and-sunshine sort of guy."

A couple of minutes later, after finding a pair of shoes, combing her hair and applying a quick dab of lipstick, Priscilla led Cowboy out of the brownstone. He waited as she locked the door, then they headed toward the neighborhood park.

"What did you find out?" she asked.

"You were right about the name change. Your father was born Clifford Richard Epperson and never made Clinton Richards legal."

"So my name is actually Priscilla Epperson?" she asked.

"Yep."

"What about the birth certificate I gave you? It gives our names as Richards."

"The birth certificate was a good copy, but it was a fake. Someone paid to have it created."

Reality slammed into her chest, and she had a difficult time catching her breath, let alone coming up with a response. Her life had been a lie. Counterfeit. Or so it seemed.

They continued to walk as she waited for him to tell her what else he'd discovered. Her pumps and his boots made a harmonious crunch and tap as they continued down the sidewalk.

When it became apparent that he wasn't busting at the seams to talk, she spoke up. "What else did you learn?"

"Your father was born and raised in Cotton Creek, Texas. That's where he and your mother lived up to and after your birth."

"I've never heard of it. He said we used to live in a little Podunk town about two hours outside of Austin."

"Actually," he said, "Cotton Creek is closer to San Antonio."

Oh, God. Her father had lied to her over and over again. Her grief bounced between anger and disappointment.

She'd wanted to learn her father's secret, but she wondered if Cowboy had uncovered more of the past than she'd bargained for.

"Why did he change his name?" she asked. "Was he in trouble?"

Cowboy placed a hand on her back, warming her from the inside out, then guided her toward a park bench that rested in the shade. "Why don't we sit down?"

Priscilla didn't want to sit. She wanted to hear the secret her father had kept from her.

It seemed as though Cowboy wanted to break it to her gently, and she appreciated his thoughtfulness, but she was a lot tougher than he realized.

Her circumstances might look different to an outsider, but over the past twenty years she'd been taking care of her father, not the other way around.

Cowboy nodded toward the bench. "Have a seat."

Instead of arguing and telling him to cut to the chase, she complied like the obedient child she'd always been. The child who'd tried desperately to make life easier for her father. A man who'd lied to her.

"What do you know about your mother?" he asked.

"Not much. She and my dad were high-school sweethearts. And she died when I was three. Her name was Jezzie. But then again, maybe he lied about that, too."

"Your real birth certificate lists his wife as Rebecca Mae Epperson."

Priscilla was glad she'd taken his advice and sat down. Her knees would have given way had she been standing.

"Are you sure about that?" she asked.

He nodded. "Yep. And Rebecca Mae Epperson is still living in Cotton Creek."

Reality slammed into her chest like a fist, and a knot formed in her stomach. She found it hard to breathe, hard to speak.

For the longest time Priscilla couldn't seem to grasp what Cowboy had told her.

"My mother is alive?" she finally managed to ask. "What about the fire?"

"I don't know anything about a fire. But from what I've gathered so far, your father was accused of a noncustodial kidnapping."

Oh, dear God.

Her pulse pounded in her head. And although she wanted to deny it, to call Cowboy a liar, to scream obscenities and run back home, she knew in her heart what he'd just told her was true.

She blew out a wobbly sigh as she pondered the first of her father's lies. "He told me that we left my mother behind to wait for the moving van and take care of odds and ends. She was going to fly to Rapid City, where we were supposed to take her to our new home. But the night before she was to leave, while I was asleep, he claimed to have received the call about the fire. The news of her death."

But it had all been a lie.

A tear slipped down her cheek, and she brushed it away, only to have it replaced by another. Her lip quivered, and she bit down to hold it still. To hold herself together.

It was too much.

She didn't have the foggiest idea what to do next, where to start. So she turned to Cowboy for direction.

"Now what? Where do we go from here?"

Chapter Three

Where do we go from here?

We?

Damned if Cowboy knew. But Priscilla was looking at him as though he had all the answers.

"It depends," he told her.

"On what?" Her eyes filled with tears, and she tried to blink them back, although it didn't do much good.

"I guess it depends on how you feel about contacting your mother."

"I know. And I need to do that. It's just…" Her breath caught and she blew out a weary sigh. "I don't know what to say. Or how to go about it. What am I supposed to do, just show up at her front door and announce that I'm her long-lost daughter?"

"You can check and see if your mom's phone number is listed, then call and let her know you're alive and well."

"And then what?" She was looking to him for advice, and he'd be damned if he knew what to suggest or what she might be able to handle.

This was just what he'd been afraid of—having her fall apart, then him not knowing what to do, what to say.

He thought about Jenny, about the way he'd failed her when she'd needed him most, and his chest constricted. He wanted to bolt—not just from the memories but from the here and now. He'd never been up for the heart-to-heart stuff. And over the years he'd developed a happy-go-lucky philosophy that had served him well.

Besides, his work on this case was done—for the most part. He'd uncovered the truth about her old man's identity. And now he wanted to pass the baton to someone else, to let Priscilla's friends support her from here on out. There had to be a slew of others who were more capable than he was.

But when she looked at him with the most expressive eyes he'd ever seen, tear-glistened and the color of bluebonnets, he was stuck.

And like the spinning wheels of a Chevy pickup resting bumper-deep in a mud hole, he was just as immobile.

He had to figure out a way to dig himself out of the muck and mire, to find a quick fix, to get Priscilla back on track.

It was the only way he could appease his conscience while he cut bait and run.

"Let's take some time to think this through." He stood, slowly turned and reached out a hand to help her up. "Come on, I'll buy you a sarsaparilla."

Her hand, small and delicate, slipped into his, and she got to her feet. "What's a sarsaparilla? Isn't it a root beer?"

"Yep. But I was only using it as a figure of speech. I'd prefer the real thing. How about you?"

"You mean a beer? I don't like the taste. Actually I'm really a teetotaler, but a glass of wine might take the edge off what's turning out to be a bad day."

She released his hand, then walked beside him, something that was both nice and unsettling at the same time.

The wind whipped the strands of her hair and kicked up the faint scent of something floral. Lilac, he guessed.

Whatever it was, he liked it.

A little too much.

For a man prepared to hightail it back to the comfort of his office as soon as his conscience would allow it, he was finding it much too easy to stay in step with the pretty redhead.

And God knew he didn't need to get involved

with a client or get sucked into the emotional struggle she was dealing with.

"You know," he said, hoping to take a detour on reality. "You don't need to decide anything today."

"You're right. There's been a lot to think about, a lot to consider." She glanced up at him, a myriad of emotions brewing on her heart-shaped face.

He suspected she was angry at her father. That was a given. And she had to be hurt, confused. Looking for support, comfort.

Surely she didn't expect anything out of him. Dealing with emotion had never been his strong suit. And then there was Jenny. When she'd needed a shoulder to cry on…

Damn. Been there, failed that.

Still, in spite of feeling like a greenhorn when it came to this kind of thing, he couldn't very well take her back home disillusioned and wallowing in sorrow.

When he'd first walked into her house, he'd noticed the shades drawn, smelled the stale, musty odor of days gone by. And all he could think of was getting her out of that mausoleum and into the sunshine.

Taking her back there was out of the question until he was sure she'd be okay alone.

Maybe if she had some time to let the news settle, she'd accept her father for what he was—a real son of a bitch, as far as Cowboy was concerned—and get madder than an old wet hen. Her anger would be a hell of a lot easier to deal with than her tears.

The sun warmed his face as birds chirped in the

treetops that lined the edge of the park they were leaving behind.

He wasn't sure if a drink would help her, but it would certainly help him. He'd never been one for hand-holding and soul-baring, so he'd welcome anything that would get them through the next hour or so.

As they walked along, she bumped her shoulder against his arm in an intimate manner, as though they'd been friends for a long time.

Jenny used to do that—wander a bit too close, nudge him to get his attention, tug at his shirtsleeve.

The reminder struck unexpectedly, and he struggled to get his mind back on an even keel.

"So," he said, leading her from the park. "Where's the nearest bar?"

"Riley's is only a couple of blocks away."

"Perfect." He'd buy her a shot of courage, then suggest she either call Rebecca Epperson in Texas or a trusted friend. That way she could forget about the loss of her father and his lies while either renewing a relationship with the mother she never knew or getting on with her life.

Then Cowboy would be able to leave his client in better shape than he'd found her.

That ought to appease his conscience, the crusty old troll that lived deep in his soul and cropped up every once in a while to remind him that it hadn't been his mother who'd caused Jenny's death.

It had been him.

* * *

In a dark corner of Riley's—a small local bar that was nearly empty at three in the afternoon—Priscilla sat across from Cowboy.

She nursed a white wine as he took a swig of his second beer.

"You're a lightweight," he told her, nodding to her nearly full glass. "And it's going to take more than a couple of swallows to take the edge off the day you've had."

She rolled a corner of her cocktail napkin, then locked her gaze on him. "I'm not going to drink myself into oblivion over this mess, if that's what you're suggesting."

"I'm not trying to get you drunk. Heck, I'd hate to have to carry you out of here."

"You could have fooled me."

"What do you mean?"

"You suggested I start with a shooter. And that would have sent me under the table. I'm not used to alcohol and I haven't had anything to eat all day other than half a bagel at breakfast."

He shrugged, his lips quirking in a crooked grin. "Just trying to help."

Getting drunk wasn't a solution or an option, but she still appreciated his attempt to get her mind off her troubles. She'd become pretty self-sufficient while growing up; she'd had to be. And it was nice to have a man offer her the emotional support she hadn't received from her dad.

For some reason—a reason she was just now beginning to grasp—her father had withdrawn more and more over the last few years, even before the liver cancer had been diagnosed. He'd worked at home designing Web sites, a job that allowed him to distance himself from his clients and the real world. Over time he'd almost become a hermit, which had worried her.

For as long as she could remember, she'd felt compelled to look out for him, to protect him. And to be honest, his growing attachment to her had become a concern.

"I loved my dad," she admitted. "But that doesn't mean I'm not angry at him."

Cowboy nodded as though understanding her completely.

"A week ago I was dealing with the grief of loss, thinking it would get easier over time. But I'm not sure I'll ever get over his deceit."

"It must be tough to realize someone you loved and cared about wasn't the kind of person you thought he was."

She sought his gaze, his understanding. "Have you ever had that happen?"

"People have let me down and tried to deceive me," he said. "But I've never had to deal with anything like this. Still, I have a feeling that once you talk to your mother, you'll see light at the end of the tunnel."

Maybe.

She hoped so.

She lifted her glass and sipped the wine, relishing the cool splash along her throat, growing used to the taste.

"You know," she said, "it's hard to comprehend what my dad did to my mother. I can't imagine what drove him to it or the pain he must have caused her."

Cowboy took another swig of his beer, but his attention seemed to remain focused on her, on her struggle. She appreciated his support more than he would ever know.

And he was right. She needed to talk to her mom, to learn the truth. To set things straight.

Cowboy reached into his pocket and pulled out his cell phone. "Just out of curiosity, let's see if there's a Rebecca Epperson listed in Cotton Creek. From what I've learned, it's a pretty small town."

He flipped open the lid and dialed four-one-one. No luck.

Then he asked for the Cotton Creek chamber of commerce. Moments later, after connecting with the person who answered—someone who seemed to be awfully chatty—he pulled out a pen from the inside pocket of his leather jacket and scratched out a number on the dry edge of his damp cocktail napkin.

After the call ended, he looked at Priscilla. "She suggested I call the Lone Oak Bar."

"Why is that?" Had her father's selfish act caused her mother to turn to alcohol, to become a regular at local watering holes, where she drowned her sorrows?

"The gal who answered the phone—a talkative woman who claimed to have been born and raised in the community—said Rebecca Epperson owns the place."

In her dreams Priscilla had imagined her mother as the cookie-baking, quilt-sewing type. But a businesswoman? And a bar owner?

She took a drink of wine and then another. As she finished the glass, a numbness began to settle over her, and she welcomed the calming effect as well as the buzz.

There was so much she didn't know, things that shouldn't have been kept secret.

Had her mother been a victim? Or did the secret go deeper than one parent's selfish act?

The investigation, she suspected, had only just begun.

Cowboy slid the napkin to her, then placed his cell phone on the table and pushed it forward. All she had to do was pick it up, which sounded easy enough. But it wasn't.

"There's something weird about calling my mother for the first time from a bar," she said.

"I don't know why. She'll be talking to you from one."

"That makes it even worse." She fingered the stem of her glass, then took another drink. "Besides, when I talk to her I want to do it in person."

And she didn't want to do it alone.

She looked at Cowboy, unsure of how he'd react

when she asked him to go with her—as part of the job.

Maybe they could hang out in Cotton Creek for a day or two, drop by the bar her mom owned. Check out the woman from a distance. After all, maybe her father had left her mother for a good reason.

What other secrets would they uncover in Texas?

Priscilla reached across the table and placed her hand on his forearm. "I want you to go with me to Cotton Creek."

"Me?"

The jolt of his reaction, as well as the warmth of his arm, the bulk of his muscle, caused her heart to skip a beat, and she pulled her hand away, breaking the brief but captivating physical connection. "I'll pay you for your time, of course. But I feel totally out of my league. And I'm not sure what I'm up against. What if my mom isn't a good person? What if there's a lot more to the story than we've been able to piece together? What if my dad thought he was protecting me?"

"Protecting you from what?" Cowboy asked.

She shrugged. "I don't know. Maybe my mom was abusive."

"Do you remember her hurting you?"

"No, but I can't remember much about her. Not even what she looks like."

Cowboy motioned for the bartender.

"What are you doing?" she asked.

"Getting you another glass of wine."

She started to object but blew out a sigh. Why not have another glass? It was not as though she had to finish it. And if truth be told, she relished the calming numbness the last one had provided.

The bartender brought them the round Cowboy had requested as well as a white ceramic bowl filled with mixed nuts and placed them on the table.

"I really shouldn't have any more wine," she admitted. "But you're right. It has helped. And I actually like the taste."

"Good." He reached into the bowl and grabbed a handful of nuts, then popped them into his mouth.

"So," she said, drawing him back to her original request. "Will you go with me to Texas? I really don't want to confront my past alone. And I have a feeling I'll still need your expertise."

Cowboy didn't think going with Priscilla was a good idea, although he couldn't put his finger on why. The fact that he ought to backpedal on his involvement with her rather than allow himself to be pulled in deeper, he supposed. "What about your friend, Byron Van Zandt's daughter?"

"Sylvia? She was just promoted at work and she can't take any time off right now. Besides, I'd feel better if I had a private detective with me, someone who could do a little investigating on the side, if necessary."

"I...uh..." Damn. Why was he hemming and hawing? It was just another job. No big deal.

And besides, Cowboy had no idea what had provoked her father into leaving town and changing their names. She was right. There was more work for him to do.

But traveling with an attractive, blue-eyed redhead with a bedroom voice?

If she weren't a client and so damn prim and proper, he might be inclined to consider the trip as a pleasant diversion, a vacation. Maybe even take a chance at a brief but hot sexual fling.

But that was out.

"It would only be for a few days," she added, placing her hand on his arm again, sending another rush of heat through his veins and stirring up the rebel in him.

She was putting him in a hell of a fix. Part of him demanded he sail off into the sunset, while another part begged him to jump ship before the storm hit.

But when she looked at him with pleading eyes, he buckled.

Aw, what the heck.

"Sure. I'll go." He picked up his cell, then called Margie at the office, asking her to book him and his client on a flight into San Antonio tomorrow morning.

When the call ended, he suffered a moment of doubt, an urge to hand over the case to one of his colleagues. Something told him Priscilla wasn't just another client.

He reached into the bowl, grabbed a handful of nuts and popped them into his mouth. He watched as she picked out a couple of cashews from the bowl, then ate them one by one.

"You know what?" he asked, cracking a grin. "Your name really suits you."

"Priscilla?" Her brow furrowed. "How so?"

"You're prissy. And a real girlie-girl."

"You say that like it's a bad thing."

"Nope. Just an observation." And a realization that ought to make it easier for him to steer clear of her in a romantic sense.

She took another drink, but her eyes remained fixed on his, as though waiting for him to explain.

But he didn't. He just reached for another handful of nuts, which were too salty—a trick to get patrons to drink more.

They sat in silence for a while, lost in their own thoughts, until his cell phone rang, drawing him from his musing. He answered to find Margie on the line. She'd made reservations with the airline but wanted to run it past him before purchasing the tickets.

He interrupted his telephone conversation long enough to ask Priscilla, "How about a flight out of Newark at ten tomorrow morning?"

"That's fine." She settled back in her seat and took a healthy sip of wine.

When he asked about a rental car and a motel, Margie said, "I've requested an SUV. Do you want a luxury model?"

"Not this time." If he wanted to roll into Cotton Creek and belly up to Rebecca's bar, he wanted folks to think he fit in.

"And as far as motels go," Margie said, "I'm still trying to locate something you'd be comfortable in. It's a pretty small town, so it'll be tough to find your usual accommodations. So far, I've found a bed-and-breakfast that sounds like it might do. Any objections?"

"No, that'll be fine."

Margie knew he preferred top-of-the-line hotels when possible, so he trusted her to do her best.

After he and the secretary finished their conversation, he disconnected the line.

Priscilla placed her elbows on the table, leaned forward and whispered, "Do you know where the restrooms are?"

He scanned the darkened bar, then pointed toward the east wall, where a sign was posted.

As she scooted her chair back, her knees buckled and she grabbed the table for support. Her eyes widened and she clamped her hand over her mouth. "Oops."

After only one drink? He glanced at her second wineglass. Okay, so she'd finished that one, too. Courtesy of the salty cashews, no doubt.

He supposed that was a lot of alcohol to hit a tee-totaler's system in a short period of time. And on an empty stomach. He'd hoped a little alcohol would make her feel better about things, about the crap in her past. But he hadn't planned on her getting drunk.

Heck, the women he hung out with were party girls who often started out with a shooter. But Prissy wasn't like the women he dated. And he supposed he should have known better.

"Are you okay?" he asked.

She nodded. "But I want to splash a little water on my face."

Then she walked across the scarred hardwood floor. Was she staggering a bit?

Dang. Dealing with an emotional woman was bad enough. But one who was snockered, too?

She reached back and tugged at the hem of her blue cotton blouse, making sure it lay neatly against a shapely derriere. She was a pretty woman. And it would tickle the hell out of him to see what she'd do when her inhibitions had been peeled away by the fruit of the vine.

But then what?

She was a client. And vulnerable.

He threw back another swig of beer. No need to let this go any further.

She'd suffered a rough blow today. And he couldn't very well leave her alone, not in the midst of those boxes she'd packed for the Salvation Army or with the memories of her father's past, his secrets.

The late Clifford Epperson might have deceived her and her mother, but Priscilla had loved him. And his death no doubt still weighed heavily on her mind, on her spirit.

No, Cowboy thought. He couldn't very well take her home and leave her locked up alone with her memories and the demons of the past.

Not overnight.

He glanced across the bar and spotted Priscilla returning.

Her steps were unsteady, and she listed to the left like a windblown ship on rough seas.

As she approached the table with her cheeks flushed, she flashed him a playful smile, then took her seat.

She leaned forward, a mischievous glimmer in her eyes. "I goofed."

In the restroom? Uh-oh. That could mean a lot of things, all of which he didn't need to hear about.

"I pushed the wrong button," she said, dimples forming.

Did she flush the wrong toilet? He was still at a loss. "What do you mean?"

"The vending machine. They have a lot of stuff in there. And I was trying to buy breath mints, just in case one of my neighbors could smell alcohol on me." She reached across the table and took his hand, pressing a foil packet into his palm. "You'll probably get more use out of this than I will."

Cowboy glanced at the neon-green packet. He wasn't so sure. He couldn't imagine any of his lovers wanting a bright green willy coming at them.

He looked at Priscilla, saw her eyes glimmering with humor, realized her prim packaging was coming apart at the seams.

There was a battle waging on his shoulder between a puffed-up angel with a crooked halo and a cocky little devil prepared to swing his pitchfork for all he was worth.

But decency won out.

"Come on," he said. "Why don't we head back to your home? You can pack your bags, then come into Manhattan with me this afternoon."

"Why?" She reached for her empty wineglass and tried to take a sip.

"You can spend the night at my place, then we can head to the airport together."

"I can't come home with you," she said, her cheeks turning a deeper shade of pink. "What will your neighbors think?"

"I don't give a squat what they think. It's none of their business. Besides, this is New York City— no one cares. Don't tell me you worry about things like that?"

"I…" She bit her bottom lip. "I guess it's kind of a habit. My dad had always insisted on keeping a low profile. I thought it was because he was shy and self-conscious. Now I'm wondering if that was his way to keep his secret safe."

"Listen, Prissy. You're not the first client who's stayed over. My neighbors are too busy with their own lives to give a second thought about mine. And if they're not too busy, they ought to be. Nevertheless, I have a sofa that makes out into a bed."

"You have clients spend the night with you?"

Well, she'd be the first female client. "Yep. It's all in a day's work."

He shoved the condom into the front pocket of his jeans, then motioned for the bill.

A cocktail waitress who'd just started her shift brought it to him. "Are you closing out your tab?"

"Yep." He pulled out his wallet, glanced at the total and added a tip. Then he handed her the cash. "Keep the change."

"Thanks, hon."

"Do you know that woman?" Priscilla asked, nodding toward the backside of the waitress heading toward the register.

"No, why?"

"She called you hon."

"Nope, I've never seen her before." As he waited for his pretty client to stand, her knees buckled, and he grabbed her arm. "Are you okay?"

"I'm just a bit wobbly."

"Come on," he said. "Let's get out of here."

As they started out the doorway of Riley's, she grabbed his arm and turned him around. "Thanks for being so sweet, Cowboy. You're a real nice guy."

Yeah, well, he wasn't feeling so nice. Or sweet.

The battle on his shoulder had begun all over again.

Before he could escort her outside, she wrapped her arms around him, pressing her breasts against his chest.

"I appreciate you being here for me," she said, her sultry bedroom voice settling over him.

The punchy little angel on his shoulder suggested he run like hell. But the devil's hormones were going wild.

"No problem," he said, trying to shake the scent of lilac, the feel of his pretty client in his arms.

His *vulnerable* client, he reminded himself.

"Come on, Prissy." He guided her onto the city street. "Let's go home."

"And then what?" she asked, slipping her arm through his.

Hell if he knew.

Chapter Four

Cowboy stood on the stoop of the brownstone, waiting while Priscilla fumbled through a small black purse for her keys.

He wasn't sure how she could lose them in such a small compartment. Or how she could pack so much other stuff inside.

Out came a wallet, several coupons held together with a paper clip, a business card holder, a pen—all of which she juggled in her hands.

"They're in here someplace." She bit down on her lip and furrowed her brow. Her befuddled little-girl expression was priceless.

He wondered if she got flustered very often.

When she withdrew a pack of breath mints, she seemed to forget about her task. "Oh. There they are. I had some after all." She flipped open the lid and offered him one.

"No, thanks."

She shrugged, popped several in her mouth and continued her search.

Suddenly she brightened and pulled out a single key connected to a silver heart. "Ta-da!"

"Here," he said, taking it from her. "Let me open it for you."

"Thanks. You're sweet, Cowboy."

And Prissy was three sheets to the wind. Of course, she was also entertaining and cute as hell.

A grin tugged at his lips as he unlocked the door and swung it open to allow her inside. But when she stepped over the threshold, her shoe caught on a green woven throw rug and her feet went out from under her.

"Oops."

He grabbed her before she hit the floor, his right arm holding her steady and resting under her breasts. They were full, soft. Warm.

He could feel her pulse throbbing, steady and strong.

His, too.

"Are you okay?" he asked.

"I think so." Her lilac scent stirred up a swarm of pheromones that sent his mind spinning and his blood pumping. "I'm going to have to replace that darn rug."

"I don't think it was the rug. It was the wine."

"Well, maybe so. I told you I was a teetotaler."

Yep. A real lightweight who promised to be a hell of a lot of fun this evening—if he was the kind of guy who'd take advantage of her lowered inhibitions—which he wasn't. But that didn't mean he couldn't enjoy watching the real woman peer out through an alcohol-induced crack in her armor.

As she regained her balance, she flashed him a smile, and their gazes locked. Whatever was spinning around them intensified.

"You know what?" Her soft, sultry voice settled over him in a bedroom whisper. "You have the prettiest eyes. They're a caramel color."

Her eyes were striking, too. Like a windswept field of bluebonnets.

Oh, for Pete's sake, she had him thinking like a friggin' poet. And even a charmer had his limits.

He released his hold, thinking she ought to be balanced, but she tottered, and the rug slipped on the polished hardwood entry. And again, before she hit the floor, he caught her in his arms.

"Whoa," he said, pulling her upright. Then he turned her to face him, hands holding her steady. "Be careful."

She tossed him an appreciative smile, then giggled. "You're a hero."

Not hardly. And the absurdity of her comment caused him to chuckle.

She reached up and stroked his cheek. "Did you know you have dimples?"

Yeah. He knew. But as her fingers skimmed the light bristle of his beard, silencing his mirth, his smile drifted away, undoubtedly taking the dimples with it.

Her expression sobered, too, leaving an intensity that sent his pulse racing to beat the band.

Her thumb brushed across his jaw, and his hands dropped from her arms to her waist.

Damn.

Where was that little angel on his shoulder when he needed it?

She stood on tiptoe, slipped an arm around his neck and drew his mouth to hers. So much for the angel. Apparently his blasted conscience wasn't mute; it had gone AWOL.

But what the hell. Prissy had started it.

The kiss began slowly, sweetly. Just a soft, brief moment of curiosity that led him astray. Just a zest of peppermint that drove his taste buds crazy, that sent his blood rushing. His thoughts swirling.

He'd never kissed a woman like her before, and the urge to hold on tight and savor the moment damn near swept him away.

As her lips parted, their tongues touched, sought, caressed. A blast of heat surged through his bloodstream, and he drew her close. As he ran his hands along the soft contours of her back, her hips, she whimpered and leaned into him.

Something far more powerful than fascination took charge, and he was lost in the moment, in the heat of her embrace.

As the kiss intensified, the prim and proper lady faded by the wayside, and the woman who owned that sultry voice took over, tempting him beyond distraction—until a high-pitched voice called from out on the street.

"Priscilla?"

As if on cue, the sultry sex kitten evaporated into a heated vapor and the prim children's-book editor returned.

He could taste her peppermint-laced gasp as she tore her mouth away and pushed against his chest.

"Mrs. Hendrix," she said, her voice rising an octave and her hand batting away a loose strand of hair. "Hello!"

The older woman made her way along the sidewalk and to the steps that led to the stoop like a matronly guardian of social protocol. "Is everything all right?"

Priscilla feigned a smile, yet rosy cheeks and a sexual flush on her throat boasted her embarrass-ment. "I…just…yes, I'm fine. This is…" She glanced at Cowboy and paused, eyes wide, lips parted, confusion splattered on her face.

Well, if that didn't beat all. Prissy was so flus-tered, she'd forgotten his name.

He turned to face Mrs. Hendrix—one of the feared neighbors, no doubt—and flashed her a dis-arming smile. "Trenton James Whittaker, ma'am."

"It's nice to meet you." The silver-haired woman placed a hand on her chest and fingered a button on her blue cardigan. Her gaze flitted between him and Priscilla.

Cowboy had never been one to give a damn what people thought about him, so he couldn't understand Prissy's concern, her hesitation, her embarrassment. Hell, the neighbor probably didn't even give a squat anyway.

But for some reason, chivalry stepped in to fabricate a lie that would get his client off the hook. "I'm Prissy's cousin."

"I…uh…we were…" Prissy looked from Cowboy to Mrs. Hendrix and back again. It didn't take a brain surgeon to figure out she'd probably never lied a day in her life, not even to save her butt from a well-deserved swat as a kid.

"We were just getting caught up," Cowboy supplied. "It's been years since we've seen each other, and I was just passing on a hug and a kiss from everyone on my side of the family."

"Well, now, isn't that nice," Mrs. Hendrix said.

"I'll be taking Priscilla home with me," he told the woman. "To be with family in Texas."

Mrs. Hendrix looked at Priscilla for confirmation. Or possibly an explanation. "But I thought you were from Iowa."

"She is," Cowboy said. "But *I'm* from Texas. And so is my side of the family."

The woman laughed. "Well, for goodness sake. You didn't need to tell me that, Mr. Whittaker. Your accent gives you away. And so do the hat and boots."

"I suppose I do stand out like a sore thumb in these parts," Cowboy said, playing the role to the hilt, as he often did. "In fact, ma'am, the sooner I can get back in the saddle, the happier I'll be."

Then he gave Priscilla a love pat on that pretty little backside of hers. "Cousin Prissy, we're burnin' daylight. Go on inside and pack your bag."

"If you'll excuse me?" Priscilla said, taking the escape route he'd given her.

"Of course, dear. Have a nice trip."

Cowboy flashed Mrs. Hendrix a charming smile— one of his best. "It was nice meeting you, ma'am."

"Likewise." She smiled, then slowly turned around and shuffled back to her own place.

He ought to have been glad the neighbor had gone, leaving the two of them alone, but he wasn't.

Not at all.

That kiss had been a complication he'd have to put behind him pretty damn quick.

What in tarnation had he been thinking? He didn't kiss women who had more than a good time on their minds. And he didn't take advantage of vulnerable clients.

But after seeing Prissy's playful side and tasting her kiss, he'd gone from being attracted to a client to being tempted by one.

And that could mean trouble down the road if he didn't watch his step and keep his hormones in check.

* * *

Priscilla perused the spacious loft apartment that Cowboy called home, taking in the hardwood floors, the trendy furniture, the plasma television, the expensive stereo system—surround sound, she guessed.

Colorful paintings—interesting pieces that looked like originals rather than prints—adorned the cream-colored walls.

She didn't know what she'd expected. A Southwestern decor, she supposed. Maybe Native American art on the wall. Something that reflected his Texas roots the way the sound of his voice did.

There was more to the man than met the eye, she supposed.

Still, she spotted the usual masculine clutter: a *Sports Illustrated* on the coffee table, a *TV Guide*, a couple of crushed beer cans on the counter rather than in the trash. But other than that the place was orderly and clean.

She slid a glance at Cowboy. Surely he wasn't that tidy.

Her father certainly hadn't been, especially the last couple of years, when he'd begun to withdraw more and more from society. He used to leave crossword puzzle books, candy wrappers and newspapers all over the house. Of course, that was about the time their roles had reversed and she'd begun looking out for him.

Until recently she'd assumed he'd never recovered from the loss of her mother, that he'd been grieving himself to death.

But now she knew that wasn't the case.

Cowboy placed her suitcase on the floor next to the glass-top coffee table, then offered her a seat.

She chose a state-of-the-art beige recliner. "You keep your place clean."

"Thanks to Marguerite, who was here yesterday." He tossed her a smile, then sank into the cushions of a black leather sofa and draped an arm over the backrest.

"You know," Priscilla said, "I can't believe I let you talk me into this."

"Talk you into what?"

"Coming here to spend the night."

He shrugged. "You weren't in any shape to be staying home alone."

"Maybe not an hour ago. But I'm feeling much better now."

By the time they'd climbed out of the subway and headed down the street to his apartment building, Priscilla had begun to sober.

Of course, the memory of the heady kiss they'd shared hadn't abated. And if truth be told, it was still doing a number on her.

The entire embrace had been surreal, out of this world. And so had her brash behavior.

Had she really slipped her arms around the handsome private investigator's neck and instigated a kiss?

It was *so* not like her, and she feared she'd given him the wrong impression.

Did he think she planned to continue drinking and really tie one on later this evening? Or that she planned to share his bed?

She hoped not, since there was no way she'd let things get out of hand again. And the sooner he understood that the better.

So as a reminder of their sleeping arrangement, she asked, "Are you sure you don't mind me staying the night on your couch?"

"Not at all. It'll give us a chance to get an early start in the morning."

He was probably right. Besides, it would have been a miserable night to spend alone—drunk or sober. She had too much to contemplate, and there were too many hours before dawn to do so.

Yet staying with Cowboy was going to be awkward at best. Especially since that darn kiss still hung over them and would continue to do so until she addressed the issue.

She opted to face it head-on. "I apologize for kissing you like that. It won't happen again."

A grin tugged at his lips, and his eyes glimmered with mirth. "I figured it wouldn't."

He had? "Why not?"

"Because you're too prim and proper, for one reason. And you worry too much about what people think, for another."

"You say that like it's a bad thing. I've worked hard to build a good reputation."

"And even harder to put up a good front."

His words ruffled her pride. "What do you mean by that?"

"You're uptight and don't know how to have fun."

"I know how to enjoy myself," she said.

"Doing what?"

"Reading. Going to the museum. Seeing Broadway plays. Hanging with Sylvia after work." She sensed he wasn't impressed.

"You never color outside the lines, do you?"

"No. That's not the way I do things." She brushed imaginary lint from her lap. When she looked up and caught his gaze, she spotted a humor-filled glimmer in his eyes.

He'd just been teasing, she supposed.

But had he also been reminding her of their differences and why they might never kiss again?

She really had no desire to stir things up with him in a romantic sense, but the thought of kissing him again was tempting.

"Are you hungry?" he asked. "There's a deli on the corner and an Italian restaurant just down the street. There's also a guy with a sidewalk stand on the next block with great hot dogs, if you're up for something like that."

"I skipped lunch today, so I'm ready to eat. And as for where, it's your call."

"In that case, let's go to Rossi's. It's a family-owned-and-operated restaurant that offers great food and entertainment."

A meal and entertainment? Gosh, that sounded a lot like a date.

"You don't need to take me to a place like that," she said. "After all, we're just biding our time until we can fly to Texas and investigate my past. Maybe we should go to the deli you mentioned."

He stood and she followed suit. But instead of heading for the door, he made his way toward her.

Uh-oh. Her senses went on red alert. Her heart rate accelerated and her breathing deepened as his musky scent, along with the rush of sexual awareness, fluttered between them.

Back away, a small, rational voice whispered. *Think of something clever to say, something safe and platonic.*

But her voice and her feet weren't listening.

The memory of that kiss spurred on a rush of anticipation, and she feared that if he wanted to kiss her again, she'd be hard-pressed to object.

He reached out and cupped her cheek. "I told you before, I'm a people watcher. I'm good at reading folks and spotting their nervousness, their guilt."

Was he talking about her?

His thumb caressed the skin above her jaw. "Don't fret about the kiss, Prissy. It was no big deal. I've already forgotten about it."

Her lips parted in surprise, then she managed to say, "Good."

In fact, it was a big relief that he'd put the kiss behind him.

Or was it?

A pang of disappointment settled over her as she realized the hottest, most arousing kiss she'd ever shared had only been memorable to her.

He dropped his hand to the side and flashed her a charming smile. "When I mentioned entertainment, I was talking about the variety of people who frequent those places. They're always sure to provide me with a chuckle or two. Come on, I'll show you what I mean."

"All right." She grabbed her purse, intent on putting the kiss behind her, too.

But she couldn't forget his taste, the feel of his lips on hers, the arousing caress of his tongue.

And even though she was determined to put it out of her mind for good, too, the heated memory followed her out the door, down the elevator and onto the street.

The quaint Italian restaurant sat only a block from Cowboy's place and had become a favorite of his. But not just because of the authentic homemade food. There was something about the hardworking, down-to-earth, tight-knit Rossi family that appealed to him.

He wasn't sure what it was, but it went beyond the pleasant laugh that jiggled Carlo Rossi's oversize belly or the warm hug Maria managed for her favorite customers.

The immigrant couple had opened the restaurant

nearly twenty-five years ago, and it hadn't taken long for the eatery to become popular, especially with the locals. And even though things really got hopping on Friday and Saturday nights, Maria and Carlo still found time to slip out of the kitchen for a brief visit in the dining room with their favorite patrons.

Their older children, Sofia and Alfredo, waited tables and pitched in wherever necessary. Even ten-year-old Mario, when he wasn't working on his schoolwork in the back room, took on busboy duties.

The Rossis were *buena gente,* as Cowboy's Spanish-speaking friends in Texas would have called them. *Good people.* The kind Cowboy liked to spend his leisure time with.

Some of the others in the Whittaker family wouldn't feel the same way. They might hire people like the Rossis or eat dinner in their restaurant, but they didn't hobnob with anyone who wasn't a regular on the Society page of the newspaper.

That snobby, highfalutin attitude, of course, was just one of the things that set them apart from the family black sheep.

As Cowboy held the door, Priscilla stepped inside the dark-wood-paneled restaurant. Alfredo greeted them in the entry and escorted them to a table where a red candle flickered from its perch in an empty wax-dripped wine bottle that had once held Chianti. He handed them menus, then told them he'd be right back.

Moments later he returned with two glasses of water and a basket of bread wrapped in a white cloth.

"It's good to see you again," the young man said before leaving them alone.

Cowboy glanced at his companion, saw her downcast expression and knew she was still struggling with the news of what her father had done, with the uncertainty of her future. And Lord knew he didn't want to spend the evening tiptoeing around the subject.

"You know," he said, "there are a lot of unknowns in this equation. But once you get to Texas you'll be in a better position to understand what really happened in the past and to plot out a game plan for the future. Stewing about it tonight isn't going to do you any good."

She glanced up and offered him a wistful smile. "You're probably right. But it's not easy to forget that my life is on end right now."

"I understand. But why not give yourself permission to think about it tomorrow?"

"I suppose that philosophy worked for Scarlet O'Hara."

Cowboy wasn't entirely sure who she was talking about. The woman in *Gone With the Wind*, he suspected. But it sounded as though she was considering his suggestion, so he took the basket, opened the linen cover and offered her first choice of the fresh-baked bread.

She picked a slice with sesame seeds sprinkled on the crust, and he chose the focaccia—his favorite.

He watched as she took a bite, then closed her eyes and voiced her delight. "Mmm. Ooh. Yeah."

With that sexy voice of hers uttering guttural sounds of pleasure, he imagined her in bed, her red hair splayed on a pillow, eyes glazed with desire, nails clawing at his back as she climaxed.

Damn. He had no business letting his mind wander in that direction.

"This is wonderful," she said, tearing off a piece of the crust. "If the entrées taste this good, you made an excellent choice of restaurants."

"You won't be disappointed. Maria makes the pasta and bread from scratch every day." Cowboy poured olive oil onto a small plate, then added a dab of balsamic vinegar. He offered it to Priscilla as a dip.

"Well, look who's here," a familiar booming voice said as the jovial proprietor made his way from the kitchen and wiped his hands on a marinara-stained apron that had been crisp and white just hours ago.

"Hey, Carlo." Cowboy stood and reached out a hand in greeting. "You're moving pretty good these days. The last time I was here, that gout was giving you fits."

The short, stocky man blew out a "whew" that whistled and shook his balding head. "I'm doing much better now, thanks to the pills my doctor gave me."

Maria Rossi, who wore her silver-streaked dark hair in a neat bun and stood a good three inches taller than her husband, slipped away from the kitchen and joined them. "We were wondering what happened to you. Welcome back." Then she turned to Priscilla and smiled.

Not wanting anyone to assume this was a date, Cowboy introduced his companion as his client.

The reminder, he decided, was more for his and Priscilla's benefit. It was best to keep their business arrangement in mind, especially as it got closer and closer to bedtime.

"Cowboy is one of our favorite customers," Maria told Priscilla.

"You say that to anyone who frequents this place on a regular basis," he responded. Yet he was still pleased with the attention.

Maria chuckled, then patted him on the shoulder. "Maybe so. But we missed you. And it's good to see you back."

"It's nice to be back," Cowboy said, taking his seat. "I was on an assignment for a couple of weeks and then Rico had a wild hair and got married. While he was on his honeymoon, he left me in charge. And now that he's home, I can kick back and have a little fun."

Not long after the Rossis excused themselves and returned to work in the kitchen, their college-age daughter took their orders.

Sofia Rossi wasn't what you'd call pretty, but her sweet disposition had an appeal in and of itself.

Priscilla chose the pasta primavera and Cowboy asked for the New York steak—medium rare—with a side of pasta.

"How's that summer class going?" Cowboy asked Sofia, who'd just wrapped up her second year at NYU with an undeclared major.

She flashed him a bright-eyed grin. "Thanks for the recommendation, Mr. C. You were right. I'm *really* enjoying psychology and plan to take two more courses in the fall. I think I've finally found a major."

Cowboy grinned. "Glad to hear it."

"Well," the young woman said, "I'd better get your order turned in. We're expecting a party of eighteen soon, and things are going to get busy."

When she'd returned to the kitchen, Cowboy's attention focused on his tablemate. On the way the candlelight brought out gold highlights in her autumn-colored hair.

She hadn't done anything but run a comb through it today, yet she seemed to grow more attractive in a romantic setting.

Maybe they should have hit the deli for takeout.

"The Rossis seem like very nice people," Priscilla said, drawing him from his thoughts.

"They're great. You won't find too many families like them. It's one of the reasons why I like to come in here."

Priscilla grinned as though he'd revealed something he hadn't meant to. And he supposed he had.

"Is that because they remind you of your family?" she asked.

"Not a bit." His quick response to her question

had been another slip of the truth, although he doubted she'd pick up on it.

But the Rossis couldn't be any more different from the Whittakers. They were demonstrative and up front with their feelings—anger, humor, love. And they were sincere.

"Sofia called you Mr. C," Priscilla said. "Why's that? Your last name is Whittaker."

He shrugged, a grin tugging at one side of his mouth. "After Rico's first visit here, he referred to me as Cowboy. And little Mario, who's been taught to use surnames, got confused and called me Mr. Cowboy. Rico thought it was pretty funny, and before the night was over they were all calling me that. And somewhere along the way it was shortened to Mr. C."

Prissy dug in to the bread basket again. "You sure have a lot of nicknames. Does anyone ever call you Trenton?"

"Up until she passed away last summer, Mrs. Petzel used to."

"Who's she?"

"My old Sunday school teacher. But that was a long time ago."

Priscilla leaned forward, her elbows braced against the table—casual, relaxed and just barely polite by Virginia Whittaker's standards. "Tell me about your family."

He wasn't sure how to respond. He didn't discuss things like that with clients. Or with anyone, for that matter.

Although once when he and Rico had shared a couple of beers, celebrating the wrap-up of a difficult case they'd both had to work on, Cowboy had opened up and spilled his guts. He wished he hadn't, though, since he'd been skating around that crap for as long as he could remember.

But his pretty, red-haired dinner companion seemed to hang on to his every word, grasping for some image of the all-American family she'd missed out on having.

"There's not much to tell," he told her. "They're all in Dallas, and I'm here."

"Are you close? Do you get to see them very often?"

"A couple of times a year." And in two weeks he was heading home for a fancy dinner party he'd been urged to attend. A social event he wasn't looking forward to. But he was closer to his sister Katie than anyone and he'd attend because it would make her happy.

Priscilla sat back in her chair and grinned. "A big family must be nice. I was pretty lonely growing up and used to long for brothers and sisters."

Cowboy had been lonely, too.

"How many kids were in your family?" she asked.

"Five. Four boys and a girl."

"And where do you fit in?"

He was the family black sheep. The odd man out.

"I'm the youngest," was all he cared to admit.

The truth was he'd been a change-of-life baby who'd accidentally been born into an oil-rich family and all the expectations that had entailed. Of course, there'd also been that nightmare pregnancy and delivery his mom had endured, the spinal block that hadn't completely taken effect, the emergency C-section.

When he was a teenager and at the height of his rebellion, his sister Katie had told him about their mother's harrowing experience in an attempt to explain that they hadn't bonded immediately and had gotten off to a slow start.

Of course, as far as Cowboy had been concerned, his mom hadn't bonded with him at all.

But, hey, he'd come to grips with that. No big deal. And he was stronger and better off because of it.

His tablemate was grinning as though he'd revealed some touching piece of news, which made him wonder if he'd said something out loud that he'd only meant to ponder.

Fortunately the conversation was interrupted when Sofia delivered their meals, then excused herself.

Cowboy picked up the steak knife and fork, but before he could dig in, Priscilla leaned forward.

Her white blouse came dangerously close to her plate, which was piled high with pasta and vegetables and laced with a creamy garlic sauce.

"So you were the baby," she said.

"And a born maverick," he added, preferring to think of himself as a fighter, not a victim.

"I can't imagine you as a rebel," she said. "You're such a charmer now."

At times his lighthearted banter was an act, a defensive ploy. It was also an investigative technique.

She fiddled with the edge of her napkin. "You seem to be downplaying it all. But at least your early years weren't lonely."

They hadn't been anything to shout about, either. By the time TJ had come along, the other kids had all pretty much moved away or had lives of their own. His dad had been a workaholic, and his mom had gotten tired of doing the domestic routine and was knee-deep in her charity work.

He wasn't going to get sucked into telling Priscilla the truth, opening up his guts and allowing her to do the same.

Cowboy, TJ or whomever he'd become didn't deal well with emotions. Not his own and certainly not someone else's.

"Hey," he told her, nodding at her plate. "Your dinner's getting cold."

"You're right. And I'm starving." As she bit into her pasta and relished the taste of her meal, a blissful expression returned to her face. "Ooh…aah…"

That sultry voice. Those throaty sounds.

Again he envisioned her in bed—his bed—and in the throes of an earthshaking, toe-curling climax.

Great. Sex was the last thing he needed to think about.

Especially when they'd be spending the night under the same roof.

Chapter Five

Ever since they'd left Rossi's, Cowboy had been thinking about the sleeping arrangements and decided it would be best if he took the sofa. Hopefully if Priscilla was comfortable in his bed and behind a closed door, she'd fall asleep quicker, and they could make it an early night.

And that meant no more chitchat, no more questions about his family.

Once they arrived home, Cowboy immediately turned on the television to an *NYPD Blue* marathon, which had been a great way to discourage conversation.

A couple of times during the commercial breaks

he had the feeling that Priscilla wanted to talk about the upcoming trip to Texas, about her fears and worries. But he wouldn't take the bait, wouldn't quiz her or encourage her to open up.

After all, they could discuss a slew of what-ifs and maybes until the cows came home, but it wouldn't solve her dilemma.

No, it was better to wait until tomorrow, when they knew what they were up against. Or rather, what *she* was up against. Cowboy was merely a hired investigator, a bearer of news—good or bad.

So there was no reason for him to think in terms of *we* rather than *she*, although, he supposed, technically he was still on the case.

During the last commercial he left Priscilla alone in the living room and sauntered down the hall, where he dug through the linen closet for a spare blanket. Then he retrieved one of the pillows from his bed.

Marguerite, his housekeeper, had worked for him yesterday, so the room was clean and the linens were fresh.

Well, pretty much.

He'd only slept in the bed once since then. And he'd showered first.

Of course, he supposed a woman like Prissy would insist upon clean bedding—not that his was dirty, but she might catch a whiff of his aftershave rather than laundry soap.

Aw, what the hell.

He placed the blanket he'd been holding on a chair in the bedroom, then tore off the spread, changed the sheets and made it up again.

That ought to make her happy.

When Cowboy returned to the living room, he spotted his pretty client curled up on the recliner and stopped in his tracks.

She'd kicked off her shoes and tucked her bare feet on the seat. Her arm was extended, and the remote rested loosely in her hand.

Her eyes were closed. And her head, with those tousled red curls, was tilted to the side.

Had she dozed off?

Apparently.

He wondered if he should give her a nudge, tell her good-night and send her to bed. Or maybe he ought to cover her and leave the pillow on the sofa for her to use later, if she woke up.

But before he could make up his mind, her eyelids flickered, then opened.

"I'm… sorry," she said, talking through a yawn. "It's been a big day."

Yes, he supposed it had been—for her, anyway. She'd had a bombshell dropped on her and a lot to deal with. Of course, tomorrow might be a whole lot worse, depending on the rubble they would stumble on in Texas.

And depending upon the kind of person Rebecca Epperson was.

He hoped Prissy and her mom would have a

joyful reunion. But if not, he was prepared to jet his client back to New York in record time.

Either way, the sooner he could pass her off to her mother in Cotton Creek or to Sylvia Van Zandt in Manhattan, the better off they'd both be. God knew Cowboy was the last one in the world to offer anyone emotional support.

If Prissy needed to lean on anyone, it would have to be someone else.

"Do you mind if I take a shower?" she asked.

"No, not at all." He watched as she unfolded her legs, climbed from the chair and made her way to the spot where her navy-blue suitcase rested on the floor.

Instead of lifting the old, battered piece of luggage and placing it on the sofa, she knelt before it and opened the lid.

All of her clothing had been folded meticulously. Not that he was a slob when he packed. But her belongings appeared to be color-coordinated and arranged in some kind of order that would only make sense to a neurotic fussbudget.

Who went to that much trouble organizing their travel bag?

Cowboy's innate skill and interest in reading people kicked up a notch as he zeroed in on his houseguest. Prissy was proving to be enigmatic.

And intriguing.

He watched as she carefully sorted through her things and pulled out a small jungle-print cosmetic bag, a nightshirt and a pair of skimpy white lace panties.

The oversize Garfield nightie surprised him almost as much as the tauntingly small piece of silk and lace did. Did she have a bra that matched? Probably.

What else did she hide behind a prim exterior?

When she glanced up and saw him watching her, her cheeks grew rosy, her lips parted. Embarrassed, no doubt.

Eager to get back on an even keel and send Priscilla to the shower, Cowboy set the bedding he held on the sofa. "Come on. I'll show you where I keep the towels."

She carefully rearranged her folded clothing to its original meticulous order, then closed the lid.

When she got to her feet, he led her to the bathroom, then nodded to the cabinet that held clean linen. "The towels and washcloths are in there. And you'll find anything else you might need in the medicine cabinet."

"Thank you."

There it went again. That sultry voice, sliding over him in tight quarters, reminding him she'd soon be undressed.

"No problem." He did his best to shake it off as he turned and walked away. Behind him, the door shut and the lock clicked.

There. He'd done it. Gotten her out of sight.

Damn. But not out of mind.

The image came unbidden, unwelcome, yet vivid and arousing.

A beautiful redhead standing naked under the

showerhead, water sluicing over her. Steam rising. Soap sliding.

His imagination ran amok, and so did his hormones.

He slid his hands into the pockets of his jeans and felt the sharp edge of the foil packet she'd given him earlier today while they'd been at Riley's.

Wow. He'd forgotten about tucking that bright green condom away and had half a notion to toss it into the trash. But then, maybe it might be fun to tease her a little—although not tonight, of course.

Later. When it *wasn't* bedtime.

Maybe he ought to place it in his briefcase and give it back to her when the case was over. That ought to color her cheeks and provide him with a chuckle or two.

But until then he had to deal with a growing attraction to his client.

He glanced at the bathroom door. She was probably undressing now.

Damn. This was going to be a hell of a long night.

Once alone in the bathroom, Priscilla placed her makeup bag on the counter, then pulled out a thick white Turkish towel from the cupboard, along with a washcloth.

She'd tossed and turned every night for the past week, and lack of sleep was catching up to her. But still, she couldn't go to bed without taking a shower. It had become an evening ritual and—usually— ensured a restful night.

As she dug through her makeup bag, she pulled out a toothbrush. But where was the paste? It wasn't like her to forget something like that.

She ran her tongue along her teeth. Yuck. She loved the fresh pepperminty taste of a clean mouth.

But wait. Cowboy had said she'd find anything she might need in the medicine cabinet, so she opened the beveled glass door and peered inside.

He'd been right. It was packed full of toiletry essentials.

She spotted a packet holding several pink disposable razors. Two brand-new toothbrushes still in their wrappers. A floral shampoo, which was definitely not his.

There it was.

She pushed an aspirin bottle aside to reach what appeared to be an unused tube of toothpaste and accidentally knocked a small box onto the counter.

Oops. She picked it up, glancing at the label. Condoms.

Well, those were definitely his.

Sheesh.

Cowboy obviously entertained female houseguests on a regular basis—perhaps a parade of them. And apparently he prided himself on being a good host.

Was he a good lover, as well?

She imagined he was, especially if the kiss they'd shared had been a clue....

Well, of course it was. Men didn't learn to kiss

like that without having all the other skills that went along with it.

Priscilla unbuttoned her blouse, then slid it off her shoulders, folded it and laid it on the counter. She'd only had one lover before—David Wilbanks, a guy she'd met when she was in college.

Their lovemaking had been okay. Nice, she supposed. But from the things she'd read in several women's magazines, she'd suspected it could have been better. And apparently so had David.

The split had been his idea, and although she'd been surprised and saddened, she hadn't wasted too many tears over her first and only breakup.

She unhooked the front-locking clasp of her bra, then removed it and placed it on top of her discarded blouse.

David had said their relationship lacked passion. She hadn't been entirely sure what he'd meant until she'd kissed Cowboy—which had been a *real* eye-opener.

David had never kissed her like that.

Priscilla unbuttoned and unzipped her slacks, then slipped out of them.

Her thoughts remained on Cowboy, on the kiss they'd shared. The taste, the heat. The mind-spinning urge to take it a step further, to allow desire free rein.

He'd never even mentioned the kiss or his reaction to her boldness other than to tell her he'd forgotten all about it, which struck an odd chord in her chest and battered her feminine pride.

First David, now Cowboy.

Was there something wrong with her?

She and Sylvia had discussed David at length, and Priscilla had come to the conclusion that the lack of passion hadn't been her problem, but his.

So if there wasn't anything wrong with *her,* then why hadn't Cowboy, an obvious ladies' man, pushed for more or at least wanted another kiss?

Not that she was willing to make love with him, but for some stupid, totally irrational reason, she wished Cowboy would have at least tried something.

So why hadn't he?

When her clothing was folded in a neat stack on the counter, she turned on the spigot and waited for the water to heat.

Maybe the reason Cowboy hadn't thought anything about the kiss they'd shared was because he wasn't attracted to her. And maybe it also had something to do with him thinking of her as prissy.

But what was so bad about that? What you saw was what you got with her.

Or was it?

She glanced into the slowly fogging mirror, saw her naked image looking back at her. No clothes to hide behind.

Just a woman who didn't know who she really was or where she'd come from.

Up until now Priscilla's life had been a lie.

A sham.

And in less than twenty-four hours the truth was

going to unravel and her facade would fall apart at the seams.

God only knew what would be left.

Cowboy and Priscilla arrived at the airport, picked up their boarding passes and went through Security. But the closer they got to the gate, the quieter she became, the slower her steps.

"I'm sure everything is going to be just fine," he told her.

"You're probably right. One way or the other. And no matter what happens in Cotton Creek, I'll be back in New York soon and getting on with my life. So even if the secrets in my past aren't something I'll be proud of, they will be just that—in the past. Over and done."

Good. That's the attitude she ought to have. *Que sera, sera.* What will be, will be.

No need to stew about it. Or discuss it with him.

So, to his relief, the next forty-five minutes passed with ease.

As they sat in the first-class section on a 757 and waited on the tarmac for takeoff, the flight attendant made one last walk down the aisle, checking to make sure carry-on items were stowed, tray tables were secured and seat backs were in a locked and upright position.

Priscilla fiddled with her seat belt, pulling it snug.

Cowboy had sensed her increasing nervousness earlier but had refused to mention it for fear she'd unload something on him that he didn't want to deal with. He wasn't good at coddling, at knowing what to say or do. Hell, if he had been, Jenny might still be alive.

Damn, would he ever quit thinking about that? About the night he'd panicked when she'd called him in tears, saying she needed someone to talk to? About how he'd been afraid to hear any more about the brutal rape she'd experienced, and come up with some cock-and-bull story about being too busy?

About the guilt that had been almost overwhelming when he'd heard the fifteen-year-old had killed herself?

Katie, who'd been the only one in the family to sense her little brother was struggling with pain back then, had pressed him about it. And he'd leveled with her. Katie had made him feel better, insisting that Jenny's parents had been better equipped to deal with her emotional state than he'd been.

It had made sense, he supposed.

In one of his college psych classes, they'd discussed depression and suicide. And he'd realized Jenny had needed professional help.

But to this day he refused to put himself in that position again, avoiding people who needed emotional support.

Well, until yesterday.

Prissy cleared her throat, drawing him back to the present. And to her nervousness.

Yet something told him it wasn't the trip to Texas

and the meeting with her mother that had her uneasy, since she'd been clear about facing her past.

So in spite of his reluctance to get personally involved with one of his clients, he couldn't help asking, "Is something else bothering you?"

"No. Not really. It's just that…well, I've never flown before."

"You've never been on a plane? In this day and age? You've got to be kidding."

"I'm afraid not. My dad and I usually stuck pretty close to home."

Cowboy didn't know how to respond to that. With sympathy, he supposed. "I'm sorry to hear that. Traveling is an education in itself."

"I imagine it is. During the summer before my last year at college I almost went to Europe." She placed a hand on the buckle of her seat belt and fiddled with the clasp. "But the trip didn't pan out."

"You mean one of those study-abroad programs?"

"No. Sylvia invited me to go on a two-week vacation with her family, but my father didn't want me to go."

"Why not?"

"At first he said it was because of the expense, since they were going for two weeks. But then Mr. Van Zandt offered me his airline miles for reward travel and said I could share Sylvia's room, which he was springing for anyway. So it wouldn't have cost that much."

"You know," Cowboy said, "your father's compulsion to keep you close wasn't normal."

"I knew that before. But I'm even more aware of it now." She brushed her hands across her thighs, then placed them on the armrests. "Fortunately college allowed me some freedom—other than the Europe trip, of course. While at Brown, I joined study groups and did several summer internships. So even though I lived at home, I developed friendships outside of the classroom."

"Where did you meet Sylvia?"

"In an intro to biology class. Even though we came from very different backgrounds, we hit it off right away. Neither of us particularly cared for science, and we commiserated with each other. But then we decided we'd better hit the books if we wanted to pass, so we started going to the library to study together. And we've been friends ever since. We eventually even managed to get jobs at the same publishing house. Meeting Sylvia has been a real blessing."

He supposed it had been, especially for a young woman who'd been as sheltered as Priscilla. But visiting with the Van Zandts had to have been a bit of a culture shock, too.

Sylvia's parents had a ton of money and power, as the Whittakers did. But as far as Cowboy knew, the Van Zandts were more genuine than his family.

"The Van Zandts are *buena gente*."

"Good people," she interpreted, obviously understanding his Spanish. "You're right. They're the best."

She seemed to ponder the thought for a while, then added, "During school breaks I spent some time at Sylvia's house and got to know her mom and dad pretty well. Mr. Van Zandt—or rather, Byron—decided to go to bat for me and appeal to my father about letting me spread my wings and fly. And he also tried to convince him to let me go to Europe."

From what Cowboy had heard, Byron Van Zandt, a top client of Garcia and Associates, could be rather persuasive. "Apparently his efforts didn't help."

"For a while they seemed to. I sensed my father was yielding. So, knowing it would take a while to get a passport, I went to the post office and picked up the forms—just in case. But when my father saw me filling them out at the kitchen table, he must have realized I was serious about leaving. He broke down and cried, saying he would miss me too badly. So that was that. I didn't go."

"You *could* have gone anyway," Cowboy said. "You were over eighteen."

"I know, but I was uneasy leaving him alone. When I was in the elementary grades, my father was very protective. But then as I got older, he found it more and more difficult to function at home without me."

"He needed therapy," Cowboy said.

"You're probably right. I'm sorry now that I didn't encourage him to seek professional help."

The captain made an announcement requesting the flight attendants prepare for takeoff.

"You know," Cowboy said, "there had to have been more going on with your dad than him wanting to keep you close and not allowing you to have a life of your own. After all, he let you spend time with Sylvia and her parents in Manhattan."

The truth in his words seemed to take her aback, yet he could see the cogs turning, as though everything had started to make sense.

So he continued, revealing his hunch. "Seeing that passport application might have set him off. Maybe he was afraid someone would realize your birth certificate was fake."

"Oh, God," she said as the plane turned onto the runway and revved its engines. "For years I thought he was dealing with grief. But apparently it was guilt driving him—that and his need to keep me to himself, to keep my kidnapping a secret."

"That would be my guess."

As the jet engines roared to life, she glanced out the window where the scenery began to rush by.

Cowboy stole a glance at her profile, saw her brow furrow, her lips tense. He peered at her hands where they clutched the armrests.

He didn't know why he did it; it certainly wasn't his style. But as the plane began to lift off, he placed his hand over hers.

Her head turned toward him and their gazes caught. Sincerity and gratitude washed the tension from her face. She rolled her hand, palm turning upward, fingers lacing through his. Then she shot him a smile that reached deep into his heart. "Thanks, Cowboy."

He merely nodded, feeling a bit chivalrous and gallant, something he hadn't felt in a while.

A *long* while—if ever.

Once the wheels left the runway and the nose lifted, the force of their ascent pressed them back in their seats.

He could release her hand now, although for some dumb reason he didn't.

Priscilla held tight to Cowboy's hand, appreciating his support more than he would ever know. He was the kind of man a woman could lean on and share her secrets with. A man who knew just the right thing to say or do that made her feel safe and secure.

She relished the warmth of his touch, the strength of his grip, and she savored the realization that he was on her side.

It wasn't until the plane rose above a sea of cottony clouds that he slowly released his hold.

"Thank you," she said again. "I feel much better now."

"Just doing my job."

Yes, that might be true. She'd hired him for his professional expertise, but it was his unexpected emotional support that meant the world to her. It had been ages since she'd felt as though she had someone to lean on, a partner.

A handsome partner she was growing more and more attracted to.

But now wasn't the time to ponder their relationship

or even wonder if they had any kind of future together. Not until she uncovered the truth about her past.

But after that?

Her thoughts drifted to the words Sylvia had told her during the party to celebrate her promotion.

God knows your love life could sure use a shot in the tush. And believe me, Pris, this guy will do it. If I weren't involved with Warren, I'd have jumped his bones in a heartbeat.

Of course, dating or jumping Cowboy's bones was one thing. But that didn't mean the P.I. hottie would be the kind of man a woman could pin her heart on, did it?

A beveled glass door opened in her mind, revealing the contents of his medicine cabinet, the ladies' toiletries he kept, the supply of condoms.

The man was a charmer. A player. And not likely to settle down.

Okay, so Cowboy wasn't the kind of man she needed to focus her attention on in a romantic sense. But at least she could depend on him to stick by her on this trip, which gave her an enormous sense of relief.

No matter what happened in Cotton Creek, everything would be okay.

As long as Cowboy's hand was available for the holding.

Chapter Six

Margie had made their reservations at Clarissa Posey's Bed-and-Breakfast, which was located about ten miles off the interstate.

There'd been another option, the Stardust Inn. But when they'd passed it about a mile back, Priscilla was glad Cowboy's secretary had opted for the B and B.

"Here it is," Cowboy said, turning into a long, winding drive. "And it looks like a lot nicer choice than the no-tell motel we passed."

Priscilla had to agree.

The pale blue, two-story Victorian home sat upon a hill that overlooked the small town of Cotton Creek. The grounds were lush and green, the lawn well-manicured. Splashes of reds, yellows and pinks adorned the flower beds.

"It's charming," Priscilla said as she and Cowboy climbed from the rented Ford Expedition and strolled along the marigold-lined walkway to the front door.

The expansive porch held a variety of chairs and rockers that provided guests a place to sit and enjoy the fresh air and the view of the gardens. An old-fashioned swing rested near a large bay window, awaiting someone to sway away the hours.

Cowboy set down the luggage on the floorboards, then rang the bell. Moments later they were greeted by Hildegard Mullins, the owner of the B and B. Mrs. Mullins, a pleasant-faced woman, was in her sixties and wore her salt-and-pepper hair in a topknot.

"Welcome to Clarissa Posey's guesthouse." The rosy-cheeked proprietor stepped aside, allowing them entrance into a quaint and cozy sitting room where candlelight flickered, giving off a light scent of lemon.

Pale green walls were adorned with a wallpaper border that bore a delicate motif of tiny purple and yellow flowers.

Priscilla surveyed the hardwood floors and the antique furniture, including an upright piano with a crocheted doily on top. A stone fireplace sat in the far corner, with a display of old photographs on the mantel.

If one could hold memories, love and time, the proprietor of the bed-and-breakfast had. "This is beautiful, Mrs. Mullins."

"Why, thank you, dear. But let's not be formal. Call me Hildy."

"You've done a great job recreating a house from a century ago or more," Cowboy said to their hostess. "How old is this place?"

"It was built in 1888. Jebediah Emerson Posey purchased a hundred and sixty acres and moved his wife, Clarissa, to what's now Cotton Creek. He hoped the house would make her happy, since she had to leave her entire family back in Lowell, Massachusetts."

"Did it work?" Priscilla asked. "Did the house make her happy?"

"Yes, for a while. But two years later Clarissa died during childbirth." Hildy clucked her tongue and shook her head. "The poor woman was only twenty-four."

Priscilla's age. How sad.

"Jebediah was heartsick for years and never remarried. Instead, he devoted the rest of his life to his son and later to his grandchildren, all of whom were born here." Hildy surveyed her home with an appreciative eye. "The Posey house is chock-full of history. If these walls could talk, they'd tell some tales."

"How long has it been a bed-and-breakfast?" Cowboy asked.

"Nearly twenty years ago I made an offer on the house before it went into foreclosure and got a very good deal." Hildy smiled proudly. "Not everyone saw the value in this place, but I did. Of course, it took quite a while to get it renovated, but it was a real labor of love."

"It certainly shows," Priscilla said.

"Why, thank you. I wanted to keep the charm of yesteryear while providing the convenience of today."

Priscilla placed her hand on the smooth marble top of a cherrywood table and felt a chip on the side, a blemish that gave the antique character, as far as she was concerned. Yet she couldn't help wondering how it had happened, how the table was marred.

"That's one of the original pieces of furniture," Hildy said. "So is the piano, which we had refurbished ten years ago. It used to be a dark brown, but that was because the varnish had aged over the years. Originally it was a light oak, as you can see now. And you can't believe the musical tone. They just don't make instruments like that anymore."

Priscilla wondered if she'd have a chance to explore the old house. She supposed it depended upon how long they were going to stay in town.

"Why don't I show you to your rooms?" Hildy said.

"Thanks, ma'am," Cowboy said. "We'd like to get settled. And then we'll probably go for a drive."

Hildy led them to the stairway. As they followed, single file, the wood creaked and groaned in protest.

When Priscilla reached the creaky first step, she froze, her hand braced on the hand-carved banister that had been polished to a rich shine. Something—she had no idea what—compelled her to scan her surroundings, to look behind her, to the side and up ahead.

She doubted whether Cowboy or Hildy had noticed that she lagged behind, since the older woman continued to chatter away, answering his questions.

"Legend has it the house is haunted," their hostess remarked. "It's said that Clarissa Posey still wanders the halls looking for her baby. But I've never seen her."

Priscilla didn't believe in ghosts, although the stories always fascinated her. Of course, if she were to see anything that even remotely looked like an apparition, she'd probably drop dead herself.

Yet a chill had swept over her moments ago. Not a scary one. Just one that was kind of surreal.

A ghostly presence?

Or some mystical sense of déjà vu?

"Are you coming?" Cowboy asked from the top of the landing.

"Yes, of course." Priscilla shook off her uneasiness and quickly took the stairs.

When she reached the top floor, Hildy led them to their rooms, which were adjacent and on the right side of the hall. Several other closed doors lined the left.

"I'm expecting another couple tomorrow, but it's just the two of you right now." Hildy reached into her apron pocket and handed them each a schedule, giving them a brief rundown. "Breakfast is served between seven and eight. Lunch is between noon and one. There's a cocktail hour and gabfest between six and seven. And dinner is served at seven o'clock."

"Thanks," Cowboy told her.

"By the way, you requested separate rooms, but these are actually adjoining. You have a pass-through access, if you want it. All you need to do is unlock the door on both sides."

When their hostess left them alone, Cowboy carried Priscilla's bag into her room. "Let me know when you'd like to head out to the Lone Oak Bar."

"I'd like to go right away," she admitted. "But I'm not planning on introducing myself. I'd rather scout the place and check out…the people."

"Your mother," he corrected.

She nodded. "I want to watch her from a distance for a while and decide how I'm going to approach her."

And if truth be told, she wanted to decide whether she would introduce herself or not. All she needed was to learn her mom was some kind of flake who would complicate her life.

There was still the possibility—albeit remote— that her father had a good reason for leaving town with her, although she wouldn't admit that to Cowboy. Something told her that he wasn't the least bit sympathetic toward her father and would find it odd that she was.

The whole mess, she decided, was very complicated.

Cowboy placed her suitcase on the luggage

stand, then let himself out into the hall. "Just knock when you're ready. I have a hunch it'll take you forever to unpack."

"Why?"

"Because I saw the inside of your suitcase already and figure it will take you even longer to settle in than it did to pack. And if you ask me, it's got to be a pain in the butt to be so damn fussy."

"I didn't ask you."

"Then take your time. I'm on your clock." He tossed her a crooked grin, then left her alone.

Okay, so she shouldn't dawdle. But what was wrong with being neat and organized? And who wanted to wear wrinkled clothing or spend time ironing on a trip?

Not her.

She scanned her room, which was definitely decorated with a woman in mind. The walls were painted a pale pink and the windows had been adorned with white lace curtains.

Other than a lamp she suspected was a replica of an antique, most of the furnishings appeared to date back a hundred years or more.

She carefully put away her clothes, placing some of her things in the drawers of a mahogany chest and hanging the rest in a matching wardrobe.

When she was finished, she sat upon the mattress, bouncing to check the springs. She could still detect a hint of the lemon verbena sachets that lined the drawers.

Being in the Posey house was like going back in time, which was fitting, she supposed.

Because in less than an hour Priscilla would be staring her own past in the face.

Ten minutes later Priscilla and Cowboy climbed back into the rented SUV and drove toward town.

"Do you know how to get to the Lone Oak Bar?" she asked.

"Yep. While I waited for you to organize your clothes in the closet, I used my laptop to go online and check MapQuest. So sit tight and enjoy the ride."

Yeah. Right. Her palms were moist and her heart was pounding. Willing herself not to be nervous wasn't going to work.

Fortunately she didn't have long to wait or to stress.

"There it is." Cowboy pointed to a sign up ahead on the right.

The Lone Oak Bar was a clapboard building that sat in the midst of a graveled lot, between Ted's Feed and Grain and a gas station. A huge old oak tree marked the entrance, near a sign that advertised "the best dang honky-tonk in Texas."

Behind the barn-red structure sat a couple of trailers, each with a TV antenna attached. The one on the right, a green-and-white, double-wide model, displayed pots of geraniums and a bright yellow mailbox.

There weren't very many cars in the lot, just a

white Ford Taurus, a black Toyota and a blue Dodge Ram pickup with mud flaps. But Priscilla supposed it was pretty early for the party crowd.

Cowboy parked close to the entrance and turned off the ignition. "Are you ready?"

As ready as she'd ever be.

So she nodded, then climbed from the Expedition.

A blinking, flamingo-pink neon sign in the window proclaimed the bar open, which only heightened a sense of anticipation as well as apprehension.

The closer Priscilla got to the door, the louder her heart thumped, the faster it raced.

As though he could read her mind, Cowboy slipped an arm around her, pulling her close. The musky scent of his cologne swept over her, providing her with comfort and strength. "It's going to be fine, Prissy. There's no use getting nervous. If we pass ourselves off as thirsty strangers just passing through, we can head out of here at any time. All you've got to do is say the word and we'll go. No one will be the wiser."

He was right.

Still, she felt a little weird about hanging out in a bar all afternoon. But if she wanted to get the scoop on her parents, this was the place to do it.

To the side of the door, a medium-size white dog looked up from his resting spot. It wagged its tail a couple of times, thumping the wooden porch. Then it dropped its head back on its paws.

As they stepped inside, a red-and-chrome juke-box in the back played a familiar country-and-western tune—something by Willie Nelson, who'd been one of her father's favorites. Something about blue eyes, crying and rain.

Cowboy guided her to a red vinyl booth and waited while she sat and scooted inside, across a tear in the seat that had been patched with duct tape.

While he joined her, she brushed at a crumb left on the scarred and faded brown Formica table.

Moments later a pretty, dark-haired waitress walked up to their table. She was young and dressed as though she was comfortable with her body. The red tube top that didn't completely hide a vertical scar on her chest was a bit suggestive, and so were the tight-fitting jeans.

"Hey, there." The woman placed her hands on her shapely, denim-clad hips and tossed them a friendly smile. "What'll it be?"

"I'll have a Corona with lime," Cowboy told her. Then he looked at Priscilla and shot her a charming, heart-stilling grin. "How about you, hon?"

Priscilla hoped she hadn't reacted to the subtle term of endearment. And she tried not to read anything into it. She figured *babe, darlin'* and *honey* slipped easily off the hunky P.I.'s lips. He was, after all, playing a part.

Or was he?

"Do you want a glass of wine?" he asked, drawing her back to reality.

"No. I'd like a diet soda."

"You got it," the waitress said as she took off to retrieve their drinks.

Moments later the brunette set a Corona in front of Cowboy. A wedge of lime had been crammed into the mouth of the bottle. Then she placed a mason jar filled with ice and diet cola in front of Priscilla.

Cowboy surveyed the bar before addressing the waitress. "This is a nice place you have here. Looks like folks can really kick back and have some fun."

"Thanks." She tucked a long, glossy strand of hair behind her ear, revealing a silver hoop earring with a turquoise bead. "We try our best to offer our customers a reason to come back."

"Have you been working here long?" he asked.

She laughed, hazel eyes dancing. "All my life."

Cowboy arched a brow. "Heck, you don't even look old enough to drink or serve alcohol and you're making it sound as though you're an old-timer."

"Yeah, well, I turned twenty-one last week and just started serving drinks. But my mom is the owner, so you can say I grew up here, helping out whenever I could."

Her mother owns the place?

Priscilla couldn't have uttered a word if she'd wanted to.

"Who's your mom?" Cowboy asked.

"Becky Epperson." The olive-skinned beauty grinned. "And I'm Kayla Rae."

If Priscilla had found it difficult to speak before, her tongue was frozen now.

Cowboy's investigation must have turned up false information and they were going to find out that Rebecca Epperson wasn't her mother at all.

Kayla Rae, with her dark brown hair and eyes, didn't look at all like Priscilla. Or did she?

Maybe in the shape of the eyes, the cheekbones. But she appeared to be Latina or Italian.

Priscilla glanced down at the top of her forearm, at the fair skin with a scatter of freckles. No way. Surely the woman—Kayla Rae—wasn't her sister.

"So tell me," Cowboy said, nodding toward a middle-aged man and woman playing darts near the bar. "Is that lady over there your mom?"

"No, that's Thelma Hadley and her husband, Earl. They're practicing for the dart jamboree we're hosting next weekend. My mom isn't here right now. She was up all night, so she's either back at the trailer sleeping or whipping up a batch of chili."

There had to be a mistake. Rebecca Epperson couldn't possibly be Priscilla's mother.

Could she?

"Well, I'd better get back to work." Kayla Rae turned to go, then swung back around as though remembering something. "Oh! And speaking of chili, tonight is our monthly cook-off. So if you're in town and hungry, I'd suggest you either stick around or come back before seven."

"The bar is hosting a chili cook-off?" Priscilla asked.

"You bet. This place is so much more than a bar.

And you haven't tasted anything until you've had my mom's chili. The secret is the meat." Kayla Rae lifted her hand in Scout's-honor fashion. "I'm sworn to secrecy. But rumor has it that she puts in a hodge-podge of rattlesnake, horn toad and armadillo."

Priscilla scrunched her face, and Kayla Rae laughed. "You'll have to try it before making a judgment. People come from miles around to either participate in the competition or to eat their fill of Snake-adillo Chili."

When Kayla Rae left, Priscilla leaned forward and tugged at Cowboy's sleeve. "What do you think?"

"It's early yet," Cowboy said. "The jury's still out."

"Well, I'll tell you what I think. If Rebecca Epperson is my mother, then that woman is my sister. And we don't look anything alike."

"She could be a half sister. Or adopted."

"I suppose."

They nursed their drinks for a while, watching as the dart game unfolded.

Thelma, a tall, slender woman with mousy brown hair, slapped Earl's hand in a high five. "Woo-hoo!"

"Way to go, darlin'," Earl said. "You've got the touch. Nobody's going to beat us this time."

Suddenly a blond-haired boy who looked about six or seven bounded into the bar from the back and skidded across the scarred wood floor. "Kayla Rae, Mom said to tell you that Sweetie Pie is having her puppies."

"Oh, my gosh." Kayla Rae placed the tray she'd been holding on the bar. "Thanks, Tyler." Then she turned to the bartender. "I've got to go, Harley. But I'll try to come back before it gets too busy." Then she took off, right behind the boy.

"Are you as confused as I am?" Priscilla asked Cowboy. "That boy doesn't look any more like Kayla Rae than I do. And it sounds like Rebecca must be his mother, too."

"Makes me eager to meet Rebecca," he said. "And to ask a few questions. That's all."

The bartender, a big man in a red flannel shirt, walked to their table. He had a barrel chest and looked as though he could double for a bouncer. "How's it goin', folks?"

"Fine, although we're about ready for another round." Cowboy glanced at Priscilla. "You don't mind if we stick around here, do you, hon?"

"No, that's all right."

"Ready for something stronger than a soda pop?" he asked.

"No." This meeting—or rather, this stakeout—was important, and Priscilla needed to keep her wits about her. Besides, she didn't know how long Cowboy planned to play the barfly part, but this way she could be the designated driver. "I'll have another diet soda."

As Priscilla scanned the Lone Oak Bar, she spotted a mechanical bull set up in the rear, something she hadn't noticed before. "It seems as though dart tournaments and chili cook-offs aren't the only activities around here. Look at that."

"I saw it," the hunky P.I. said. "Maybe if we stick around long enough, I'll have a chance to show the Cotton Creek boys how it's done."

A scene from an old John Travolta movie flashed through her mind. "Talk about urban cowboys. I'd love to watch you get tossed on your butt by a robotic bull."

He laughed. "I'll bet you would. Maybe I ought to supply you with some salty cashews and a couple of glasses of wine, then convince you to give it a try."

Yeah. Right. "You couldn't get me drunk enough to make a spectacle of myself."

"You know something, Prissy?" He reached across the table and ran his knuckles along her cheek. "Life is going to pass you by, and you won't know how much fun you've missed."

His gesture, his touch, left her cheek tingling and set her heart on end. For a moment it was a struggle to respond, to argue.

Their gazes locked and something sparked between them.

Well, at least, she thought it had. His hand dropped so quickly she may have been mistaken.

"I'm not missing out on anything," she finally said. "I'm happy to go to a Broadway play or to stay home in the evenings and read a good book."

"That's too bad."

Before she could respond, a woman entered from the same direction Kayla Rae and the boy had run off in, and Priscilla suspected the kitchen had a back door that led to the mobile homes in back.

The woman—a short, plump brunette who wore a chambray blouse with pretty floral embroidery on the pocket and filled out a pair of stretch jeans—strode toward the bartender. "Harley, you've been defending that lazy old dog of yours for weeks. But I've got proof that he got Sweetie Pie pregnant."

"No way," the bartender, Harley, said. "Ole Whitey doesn't have enough energy to have fathered those pups. And besides, he's not my dog."

"He showed up here the day you did," the woman said, chuckling. "And the firstborn is a white male who looks just like him."

"Him showing up was just a coincidence. And besides, he'd hightail it out of here if you and Kayla Rae didn't give him his fill of leftovers."

Priscilla glanced at Cowboy, and he nodded, letting her know they were in agreement: Rebecca Epperson, the owner of the bar, had just walked in.

Priscilla could hardly breathe. She tried to spot a resemblance, either to herself or to the young woman in the photograph with her father.

Maybe.

She just didn't know for sure.

"Hey, Becky." Earl, the man playing darts, bobbed his chin in greeting. "Rumor had it you were snoozing the day away, and Thelma and I want you to know we went easy at lunch because we were planning to get our fill of your chili tonight."

"Don't you worry," Becky said. "I'll have it ready in time."

"What are you doing here, anyway?" Harley asked her. "You were up all night. You're supposed to be sleeping, remember?"

Becky placed her hands on her hips, then arched her back in a stretch. "I'll go to bed early tonight." Then she turned and strode into the room Priscilla thought was the kitchen.

"What are you thinking?" Cowboy asked.

"That I need some more time to sort things out." She glanced at the nearly empty mason jar. "And that I drank too much soda. Will you excuse me? I need to go to the ladies' room."

After seeing to the needs of her bladder, Priscilla stood at the sink, washing her hands. Before she could reach for a towel, Rebecca Epperson walked in.

"Hi." The older woman—her mother?—cast Priscilla a warm smile. "Can you believe it? I was run out of my own bathroom at home by a laboring cockapoo, a wide-eyed boy and an aspiring vet."

Priscilla managed a smile as she tried to hide her curiosity, her compulsion to spot a resemblance of some kind.

But it seemed Becky was studying her, too. "What a pretty shade of red hair. Is it your own color?"

Priscilla nodded, afraid to speak. Afraid to stutter and stammer.

"It's beautiful. I've always been partial to red hair, especially redheaded little girls."

A lump formed in Priscilla's throat, and she knew better than to talk. God help her, a public bathroom was no place to introduce herself. So she tried to conjure a grin—one of the usual responses to old ladies in the grocery store who used to make a fuss over her because of her hair color.

"Will you be here for the chili fest?" Rebecca asked as she strode toward the open stall.

"I'm not sure. I…think so."

"Good. It's always nice to see new faces around here. Are you new in town?"

"No. We're just passing through."

When Rebecca entered the empty stall and closed the pale blue plywood door, Priscilla slipped out of the bathroom. She couldn't very well hang out in there like a starstruck groupie who'd run into a famous celebrity in the head.

Suddenly she had the urge for fresh air. For some time to think. To get a game plan together.

When she reached the booth where Cowboy waited, he stood. But she didn't slide in.

"Let's go back to the B and B for a while, okay?"

"Sure. What's up?"

"Nothing. Not really. I need some time to think. But maybe we can come back tonight."

"I was hoping you'd say that." He shot her a crooked grin. "I love chili."

As they headed for the door, Rebecca's voice rang out. "Harley, I hope you're planning to get that dog neutered."

"I don't think ole Whitey would like that," Harley said with a chuckle. "There are some things a fella doesn't like to part with."

Cowboy grinned and said under his breath, "I'd have to agree."

As they headed for the door, Becky's voice rang out again. "Thanks for stopping by, folks. I hope y'all come back."

Priscilla turned and studied her mother one last time. Then she nodded.

They'd be back.

Chapter Seven

Cowboy had seen Priscilla's mom follow her into the restroom. So on the way back to the bed-and-breakfast he waited for her to tell him what had happened in there.

Had Becky recognized the daughter she hadn't seen in twenty years?

If so, Priscilla never said a word. She just sat there deep in thought and staring straight ahead.

He glanced across the console and cleared his throat to catch her attention. "What did you say to Rebecca in the bathroom?"

"Not much."

"Why did we leave the bar? You had the chance to talk to her while the place was quiet."

"I don't know." She nibbled on her bottom lip, then broke eye contact and looked at the road ahead. "When I ran into her in the restroom and she told me she'd always been partial to red-haired little girls, I nearly lost it. I was afraid she would sense something before I was ready to introduce myself. And I...well, I guess I panicked."

Cowboy wasn't sure what made her so uneasy about laying her cards on the table, although he didn't want to ask.

But if she wanted to study her mom from a distance, as she'd claimed, she couldn't very well do that from the bed-and-breakfast.

Damn. Maybe she planned to drag this on for days. And that meant he'd be stuck with her until she was good and ready to reveal her identity.

Well, not stuck. He could always bail out early.

But he felt kind of...committed. He'd always made it a point to be true to his word and he'd agreed to come with her.

Again he looked across the console, studied her profile, the red curls that looked stylishly rumpled, the thick lashes, the light scatter of freckles on a turned-up nose, lips that looked kissable in spite of a frown.

He could read people pretty well. But Prissy wasn't like most people.

"What are you really afraid of?" he asked.

The question seemed to have rolled off his tongue

without a conscious thought, which was bad enough. But the fact that it sounded like the kind of thing a shrink would ask made his gut clench.

God, what if she unloaded on him? Told him her innermost thoughts. All he needed to do was open a Pandora's box full of emotion, fears, deep-rooted insecurities…

All the crap he didn't want to deal with.

"I'm not sure what I'm afraid of," she admitted. "I know it appears that my father kidnapped me and changed our names. But I don't know these people. Can't we just investigate this mess for a while without revealing who I am—or rather, who we think I am?"

Sure, they could do that. It beat sitting on his thumbs.

"All right." Cowboy pulled into the B and B, parked and turned off the ignition. "We'll start by digging up some background information."

"How are we going to do that?"

"First by interviewing Hildegard Mullins."

Her eyes grew wide, as though he'd suggested they go back and quiz Whitey, the lazy white dog sawing logs outside the bar.

But Hildy, who'd lived in Cotton Creek for twenty years or more, surely knew something. And she struck him as the type who liked to talk about the past.

"I uncover information for a living," he reminded her. "Just leave it to me."

"You'll be discreet, though. Right?"

Obviously his prim little client didn't realize that he was in his element with this sort of thing. "Don't worry. We're just in time for the cocktail hour and Hildy's gabfest."

She looked at her wristwatch, then back at him with a question in her eyes.

"You don't have to say or do a thing. In fact, it will be better if you just sit quietly and watch. I'll have a few answers in no time at all."

"And then what?"

"Then, unless you're ready to go back to New York, we'll head to the chili cook-off."

As they walked to the front door, Priscilla elbowed his arm. "If you're planning to eat at the Lone Oak Bar, we need to tell Hildy not to fix supper for us."

"I already told her."

"When?"

"While you were unpacking and coordinating the colors of your clothing in the closet. I figured we didn't come all this way to dine with our hostess. And if we didn't eat at the Lone Oak, we'd find another restaurant in town."

Once inside the house, Hildy met them in the sitting room. She'd wheeled in a cart that held a variety of beverages as well as an ice bucket. "Can I get you a drink?"

Priscilla declined politely.

"I don't suppose you have any iced tea?" Cowboy asked.

"I certainly do." The woman indicated the settee

or one of the other antiques. "Please have a seat. It'll just take a minute."

Cowboy sat in a wingback chair, which he figured looked comfortable and strong enough to hold him. The Posey house might be interesting and quaint, but if you asked him, it was too much like a museum. Heck, everywhere he turned he expected to see a roped-off exhibit.

Prissy took a seat beside him in a delicate old rocker that looked as if it would have shuddered under his weight. Once she'd settled in, she began to sway slowly back and forth as though she didn't have a care in the world.

Hildy handed him a glass of tea on ice with a sprig of mint, then poured herself a brandy from a crystal decanter. As she strode toward a chair upholstered in a rich burgundy fabric, she asked, "Did you have a nice drive?"

"We sure did," he said. "Cotton Creek is a great little town. And the residents seem to be very nice."

Hildy took a slow sip of her brandy. "That they are. Back in the eighties, when I moved here, the community welcomed me with open arms."

"We stopped by the Lone Oak Bar," Cowboy told her. "And everyone we met was friendly."

"The people in Cotton Creek are about as good-hearted and neighborly as you'll find anywhere," Hildy said. "Who did you get to meet?"

"The Hadleys," he said. "Earl and Thelma were practicing for an upcoming dart tournament."

"Earl used to work for the Cotton Creek Savings and Loan. And Thelma is a retired nurse. Their kids have all grown and settled in another state. Missouri, I think."

"You don't say."

Hildy swirled the brandy in her snifter and watched the caramel color wash across the glass. Then she looked up and continued her spiel. "The Hadleys spend a lot of time down at the bar these days. But not because they're drinkers. It's more of a social thing for them."

Cowboy nodded. "That's what I figured. And we also met Kayla Rae Epperson."

Hildy nodded. "Now there's a smart girl. An honor student and a real animal lover. She's been attending the junior college in Clayton while working a couple days a week at Doc Crowley's veterinary clinic, and evenings at the bar. From what I hear, Doc's talked her into pursuing a degree in zoology or something like that."

"We met Kayla Rae's mother, too," Cowboy said. "If I remember correctly, her name is Rebecca."

"Everyone calls her Becky." Hildy took a sip of her brandy. "Poor gal. She's had a time of it."

"What do you mean?"

"Well, I'm not one to talk out of school, but this is common knowledge."

Cowboy wanted to hurry her along, to tell her to cut to the chase, but he knew if he bided his time, she'd open up.

And he was right.

"Becky was a Posey and grew up in this very house," Hildy said. "Why, that piano belonged to her great-grandmother. And so did the marble-topped table in the entry."

He scanned the furniture, noticing that Priscilla did, too. She was also rocking harder now, increasing her pace.

"You mentioned the house went into foreclosure," he said, drawing the older woman's attention to him and not to Prissy's efforts at stress relief.

"I hate to admit it, but my good fortune was a result of her loss."

"What do you mean?"

"When Becky hit upon hard times and couldn't pay the mortgage, I stepped in before the bank repossessed it. Not everyone was interested in an old house like this, but I was. And I snagged it for a bargain." She blew out a sigh. "I love this place and had wanted to open a bed-and-breakfast for years, but I do feel badly about Becky losing a house that had been in her family for generations."

"No one can fault you for buying something she couldn't afford to keep," Cowboy said, hoping to get the conversation back on Becky's past rather than Hildy's luck or guilt.

"Well, it was all Cliff Epperson's fault, if you ask me. That rascal was the one who coaxed her to refinance a house that was free and clear just so he could buy that bar. And then their marriage went to pot." She clucked her tongue and shook her head. "I could tell you a thing or two about *that*, too. It was a real scandal."

It didn't take much to encourage a one-sided dialogue without Hildy knowing that she was being interrogated.

"I hear you, ma'am. We've got a few stories like that back where I'm from."

"Maybe so, but I'd bet a nickel to a doorknob that this one beats any you can tell. I'd better start at the beginning."

Atta girl, Cowboy thought. Open right on up.

Her story would have her own spin on it, but at least they'd have a good idea about what really happened.

"When Becky's daddy died, he left this big old house to his wife and daughter. But two years later her mama took sick, and that slick, fast-talking Epperson boy, who didn't have a penny to his name, charmed the pants right off that poor, lonely little gal. Got her in the family way, too. And from what folks in town said, there would have been hell to pay if Becky's daddy had been alive. She wasn't quite seventeen, and Cliff was nearly thirty."

Hildy was referring to Prissy's father, a man whose real name had been Clifford—not Clinton.

Cowboy didn't dare glance at Prissy, although he suspected her rocker was about to take flight. Instead, he stuck to his game plan and leaned toward Hildy in a you-don't-say manner, and chummed their hostess into continuing her revelation, revealing how Prissy and her younger sister fit into the tale. "Kayla Rae was probably a pretty baby. She sure has grown up to be a beautiful young woman."

"Oh, no. Kayla Rae wasn't Cliff's child." Hildy stretched out her legs and crossed her feet at the ankles. "He and Becky had a little girl with red curly hair and big blue eyes. She was a pretty thing and looked just like the Posey side of the family—or so I've been told."

Cowboy struggled not to let his gaze get anywhere near Prissy's face, but he caught sight of her hands, saw the way they fidgeted on her knees.

Damn.

When he thought about what she might be struggling with, his gut twisted and he had the urge to do something.

He told himself it was because Hildy might clam up if Prissy got weepy, especially if she realized who Prissy was. He didn't think Hildy would want to share her thoughts and opinions with another Posey in the room. So he reached toward the rocker in which she sat, offering his hand, if she'd take it.

She did, and he gave it a gentle squeeze.

The warmth of Cowboy's touch, the strength of his support sent a surge of hope through Priscilla, reinforcing that she wasn't in this all alone. That she had someone who cared about her.

And Cowboy's concern couldn't have come at a better time.

Hildy's story had all the makings of a small-town scandal, and they hadn't even gotten to the part about the kidnapping.

But other than the subtle yet steady emotional support Cowboy had offered her, his focus was on Hildy and her tale.

"I sure hope Cliff was man enough to do the right thing by Becky," he said.

"Well, he married her, if that's what you mean. But I'm not so sure it was the right thing to do in this case." Hildy clucked her tongue and slowly shook her head as she caught Cowboy's gaze.

He nodded as though they both knew the secret and were on the same page. "Sounds like the Eppersons didn't have a happily ever after."

"You've got that right. Just before the first baby girl came along, Becky's mama passed on—blood poisoning from a blister on her heel that went untreated. Anyway, she left the house to Becky. And that's when Cliff started pushing her to take a loan against it so he could buy that bar. I don't know the particulars, but Earl down at the bank tried to discourage her, to no avail. But he did talk her into putting the bar in her own name."

"How did Cliff take that?"

"I don't know. But at least he got what he wanted. Of course, back then, the Lone Oak wasn't anything to be proud of. It was rough and seedy. And from what I understand, the sheriff used to get called out there regularly." Hildy took a sip of her brandy.

"That doesn't happen much anymore. Becky cleaned the place up, and not just the building itself."

Cowboy had implied Priscilla should keep quiet and let him do the talking, but she didn't care.

She stopped rocking and joined in on the conversation.

"You said the house almost went into foreclosure. How did that happen?"

"Well," Hildy said, taking the last of her brandy. "That Cliff started tomcattin' around—or so everyone says. And rumor had it that Becky decided turnabout was fair play. But Earl set me straight about that. He told me Becky took a pair of scissors and cut up all of Cliff's clothing, then threw them out on the front lawn, along with his other belongings. After that she changed the locks on the door and filed for divorce. And Earl said that was before she started dating that Rodriguez boy."

Rodriguez? That was a Hispanic name. Was he Kayla Rae's father?

If so, it explained her pretty dark hair and olive complexion. Boy, the tale was getting more complicated by the moment.

Hildy crossed her arms over her ample stomach. "When Cliff found out Becky was carrying another man's baby, he hit the roof and swore he'd kill them both. And then he went out looking for Daniel Rodriguez and found him down at the pool hall. A fight broke out, and Cliff, who'd been getting a licking, took a pool cue and darn near beat the young man senseless."

Priscilla wondered if that's where the assault charges had come from. Cowboy had mentioned there'd been a couple of outstanding warrants out on her father. One for kidnapping and the other for assault.

"Were charges pressed?" Cowboy asked.

"Yes, although there was talk about charging him with murder for a while."

"Why?" Priscilla asked. "Did Daniel die from his injuries?"

"I'm getting to that," Hildy said. "Anyway, someone called for an ambulance, but there had been a big three-car pileup on the freeway that night and the paramedics had their hands full. So a buddy insisted upon driving the Rodriguez boy to the hospital rather than waiting for medical help to arrive." Hildy clucked her tongue and shook her head. "The fool kid had been drinking all day and should never have got behind the wheel. But he did, and sped off to the hospital. He lost control of his pickup, and Daniel was pronounced dead on arrival at the hospital."

"I imagine there was an autopsy," Cowboy said.

Hildy nodded. "And the coroner ruled that Kayla Rae's father hadn't sustained life-threatening injuries from the beating but had died as a result of being thrown through the windshield."

Cowboy blew out a sigh. "You were right, Hildy. That must have been one heck of a town scandal."

"And that's not the half of it." Hildy stood and poured herself another drink. "The night after Cliff was released on bail, he broke into Becky's house and took that little red-haired girl right out of her bed. And no one has seen or heard from him since."

A knot the size of a ball and chain formed in Priscilla's stomach. She wasn't sure what to think, what to feel.

"Some folks said that Becky had brought on all the trouble herself by getting pregnant by a man she wasn't married to," Hildy said. "Well, by two men, since she wasn't married to Cliff when she conceived the first baby."

Had Hildy been one of the people who'd whispered behind Becky's back, who'd gossiped about her illegitimate child?

"But time proved them wrong."

Cowboy leaned forward. "How so?"

"Becky grieved something fierce for that stolen child. And there wasn't anyone in Cotton Creek who didn't sympathize. And then, to top it off, Kayla Rae was born with a congenital heart defect. Becky practically lived at the hospital with her, afraid to let her out of sight."

Priscilla had noticed some scarring on Kayla Rae's chest, but she hadn't realized it had been so…extensive. So serious.

"And to make matters worse," Hildy said, "Cliff hadn't made a mortgage payment in months and had run off with every penny they had to their name.

Becky had to choose between the bar and the house. And since she needed to support herself and her baby, she let the house go."

"What do folks say about her now?" Cowboy asked.

"Some say she's a saint." Hildy chuckled. "She takes in every stray and runaway that's crossed her path. Why, even Tyler isn't a blood relation, but she considers him her son."

"I guess she made the best of a tough life," Cowboy said.

"You're right. And for what it's worth, I could never imagine why she kept Cliff Epperson's name. But Thelma Hadley said it was to make sure her daughter could track her down if she ever got away from her father and came looking for her mother."

Priscilla's heart swelled to the breaking point, and tears welled in her eyes.

If there was ever any doubt before about what she needed to do, there wasn't anymore.

Priscilla was going to introduce herself to her mother.

An hour later Cowboy stood outside the bathroom door, waiting for Priscilla to finish whatever it was she was doing in there.

Thank God he didn't need to pee. All he wanted to do was shower and change.

He rapped at the door. "Are you going to be in there all night, Prissy?"

"Sorry. I'll be out in a minute."

Sharing the guest bathroom was the biggest drawback at this particular bed-and-breakfast.

When she opened the door, he stood with his legs spread and his arms crossed. His expression was one of annoyance. But when he saw what she was wearing, his jaw dropped.

"What's the matter?" she asked.

"Nothing." His eyes scanned the length of her, down to the sensible heels and back up. Not that she didn't look nice for a businesswoman. She'd swept her hair—as pretty and sexy as those curls were— into a twist.

"You're gaping at me," she said.

"You're going to a honky-tonk, Prissy. And a chili cook-off.

"So?" She glanced down at the beige slacks and jacket she wore. "I like this outfit. And I'm going to be on display. People will be looking at me. And—"

He tilted her chin with a finger, making her look him in the eyes. "And you're worried about what they'll think, about the impression you'll make."

She didn't respond; she didn't have to.

"For Pete's sake, you're dressed in business attire. What is this? A job interview?"

Cripes. In a nutshell, that's exactly what it was. Young urban professional seeking love and accep- tance.

A tear slipped down her face.

"Aw, Prissy. Don't do that." He brushed his thumb

under her eye, catching the pesky droplet. "Don't cry. You're going to end up looking like Rocky Raccoon."

She sniffled, and he had the weirdest urge to wrap her in his arms and hold her tight. To tell her everything would be just fine. But there were no guarantees in life, and the only person anyone could really depend upon was himself—or herself, whatever the case may be.

The scent of soap blended with her body lotion, bearing evidence of the shower she'd taken, of the time she'd spent in the bathroom.

She'd fussed with her hair, carefully weaving it into a perfect twist. She'd even used a touch of mascara—to thicken and emphasize her lashes— and pink gloss on her lips.

As far as he was concerned, she'd gone to a hell of a lot of effort to impress her mother.

In spite of his no-guarantees philosophy, he placed a kiss on her cheek—a move that surprised him more than it did her. "Even if you walk into the Lone Oak Bar wearing curlers in your hair and a shabby housedress, Becky Epperson will welcome you with open arms."

"You're right, but…" She didn't appear convinced.

"But what?"

"She's had Kayla Rae to love for twenty years, and I'm…the new kid on the block."

"Didn't your mom say that she's always been partial to little red-haired girls?"

She nodded.

"That has to count for something."

Heck, if Cowboy's mother had been partial to towheaded boys, it would have made his early years a lot more pleasant and memorable.

He took Prissy by the hand and led her into her room. Then he opened the wardrobe door. He checked out each garment until he found a yellow sundress and pulled out the hanger. "Here. It's still too fancy, but since I'm going to need more time to get you into a pair of tight jeans, this will have to do."

"You don't think it's too…"

"Nope." He brushed another kiss on her cheek, his lips lingering long enough to relish a second whiff of her lilac scent.

When he came to his senses, he drew away, yet those blue eyes locked on his, and he couldn't help scanning her face, her hair.

It was too prim, too proper.

He began to remove the pins she'd used, releasing those red locks and watching them tumble onto her shoulders. "You've got beautiful hair. Wear it loose tonight."

For me.

Damn. Not for him.

He had to regroup, to shake off the goofy sentiment that made it hard to breathe.

So he tossed her a reckless grin and gave her a light smack on the fanny, which was even more inappropriate than the kiss and the sentiment—but that was too damn bad.

Upon contact, her eyes widened and her lips parted. A response looked imminent, but he couldn't tell if she wanted to smack him back or laugh.

But he wasn't going to wait to find out.

"Get changed," he told her. "I'll be out of the shower and ready to go in ten minutes."

"All right."

He turned to walk away, and she grabbed his arm, drawing him back to her.

Their gazes locked, and something warm and sappy flowed over him. Something he didn't intend to mess with.

"What would I do without you?" she asked.

Her words slammed into him, making him want to duck for cover. He had to do something, say something. He had to let her know she couldn't count on him forever.

So he gently withdrew his arm from her grip. "When the time comes for me to go my own way, you'll get by just fine."

"I'm not so sure. You've been great."

Nah. Not really. He wasn't that kind of guy. Nor did he want to be.

"No one's indispensable, Prissy."

"I know that."

Did she?

He hoped so.

Because if she expected any more out of Trenton James Whittaker, she was going to be in a hell of a fix.

Chapter Eight

True to his word, Cowboy met Priscilla at the front door of the Posey house in just under ten minutes.

And even though she'd been expecting him, her breath caught at the sight of him sauntering toward her in black boots and jeans and a chambray shirt.

His hair was damp from the shower and stylishly mussed, and he carried his hat in his hand, yet his aura was true-blue cowboy.

She blew out a wobbly little sigh. The man was too darn sexy for his own good—and for hers, too.

"Hot damn, Prissy." He flashed her a crooked grin that sent her heart skidding across her chest. "That's more like it."

The fact that he'd been assessing her just as closely as she'd been studying him didn't escape her. And his blatant appreciation was unsettling yet touching at the same time.

"Thanks." She glanced down at the yellow sundress she wore, the one he'd chosen. When she looked up, he stood before her.

"You've kept your hair down." He snagged a springy curl and gave it a gentle tug. "Now all I have to do is get you to kick up those pretty heels."

His slow Southern drawl slid over her like warm scented oil and a sensual massage.

Her pulse kicked up a notch, and her cheeks warmed to the burning point. Her tongue turned to mush.

"Are you ready to go?" he asked, releasing her hair.

For another exasperating moment her words failed her again. So she nodded.

"Good. Let's get out of here."

As he slipped on his hat, Hildy strode into the room and grinned. "Now don't you two look nice."

"Thanks, ma'am." Cowboy opened the door for Priscilla, his hand resting on the knob.

"Have a good time," their hostess told them.

"We will."

Then they left the house, climbed into the Expedition and headed toward town.

By the time they returned to the Lone Oak Bar, the parking lot was full. And inside things were really hopping.

Country-western music with a boot-scootin'
beat blared from the old red-and-chrome jukebox,
while a couple of musicians set up the band near
the dance floor.

Six or seven card tables had been placed along the
perimeter, each with a Crock-Pot and ladle. A
separate table on the end held paper bowls, plastic
spoons and yellow napkins.

"Smells good in here," Cowboy said, "doesn't
it?"

"I suppose. If you like chili."

"You don't?" He looked at her as though she'd
been standing outdoors during a thunderstorm and
belting out an off-key rendition of the national anthem.

"I'm really not into spicy food."

Nor was she big on loud music.

He clucked his tongue and shook his head. "Then
you're going to stick out in Texas as much as I do in
Manhattan."

She had no doubt about that. She was completely
out of place in a honky-tonk and couldn't even
imagine life in a small town like Cotton Creek. Not
when she thrived on living in the city. "It really
doesn't matter if I fit in or not. I won't be here long."

"At the Lone Oak?" he asked. "Or in Texas?"

"Both, I suppose." She scanned the honky-tonk,
skimming over the happy faces and tuning out the
chuckles, as well as the big belly laughs, a yee-haw
and even an "I'll be go to hell."

This wasn't her idea of fun.

"Do you want a bowl of chili?" he asked.

"No, thanks. I have a nervous stomach." And at a time like this, chili would have her popping antacids like candy or running to the ladies' room.

"Then I'll eat your share." His eyes glimmered and his lips quirked in a crooked smile.

There was something boyish about the man, something endearing. And she couldn't help wondering about the child he'd been. His family must have adored him. In fact, they probably still did.

He grew serious and placed a hand on her shoulder, warming her to the bone. "Will you be okay on your own?"

"Sure. I'm just going to watch for...Becky to show up."

Gosh, what was she supposed to call the woman? Under the circumstances, suddenly referring to her as Mom seemed a bit...weird.

As Cowboy sauntered toward the cook-off, Priscilla scanned the crowd. She spotted her sister first.

Kayla Rae was dressed in another pair of tight jeans. This time, they were black denim. A pretty white blouse with lace trim completely hid the scar on her chest.

"Hey, there." Kayla Rae, holding an empty tray that dangled at her side, headed toward Priscilla. "It's good to see you back."

"Thanks." Priscilla tucked a strand of hair behind her ear.

"Can I get you something to drink?"

"No, not yet."

"Well, if you've come for the chili," Kayla Rae said, "you'll need a drink or two to put out the fire. Some of that stuff is really hot."

"Actually," Priscilla said, "I'll check out your appetizer menu instead. I'm fussy when it comes to the kind of meat I eat."

Humor glimmered in Kayla Rae's eyes. "You're not worried about eating my mother's world-famous Snake-adillo Chili, are you?"

"Let's just say that I'm not keen on reptile meat and…whatever armadillos are classified as."

Kayla Rae laughed. "Don't worry. It's part of the whole Snake-adillo Chili mystique. But just between you, me and the butcher shop, my mom can do wonders with chicken, pork and beef."

"You mean there aren't any reptiles or potential roadkill in her chili?"

Kayla Rae shook her head and laughed. "Not a single chunk. But don't tell anyone."

"What a relief." Priscilla, who was beginning to warm to her younger sister, smiled.

Kayla Rae seemed to like her, as well. Would she be equally friendly and accepting when Priscilla's identity was revealed?

"You might want to snag a table," Kayla Rae said. "They're filling up fast, and once the live music starts, people will be fighting for a seat."

"Thanks for the tip."

For a moment Priscilla thought about confiding

in her sister, about revealing who she really was and why she'd come. But it seemed only right to tell her mother first.

Of course, that didn't mean she was eager to see Kayla Rae go back to work. She wanted to talk to her a little longer. To connect on some level other than that of waitress and patron. So she asked, "How are the new puppies doing?"

Hildy's comment about Kayla Rae being an animal lover was right on target, because Kayla Rae lit up like a child facing a birthday cake laden with flickering little candles. "The puppies are *so* cute. And they're doing great. We've got four males and two females to choose from. I don't suppose you'd like to have one when they're big enough to give away?"

"I'm afraid I wouldn't be a very good pet owner," Priscilla responded. "I live in the city and work full-time."

"Which city?"

"New York."

"Wow. You're a long way from home."

Not exactly, Priscilla wanted to say. But she bit her tongue. Again she surveyed the bar, but she still couldn't spot Becky. "Is your mother here? I'd like to talk to her if she isn't busy."

"Actually my mom stayed home tonight. Tyler's babysitter canceled."

Disappointment blindsided Priscilla. She'd been so sure her mother would be *here*, so sure she could unravel her father's secret.

Should she go visit her mother in the privacy of her home?

"It's just as well that the babysitter didn't come," Kayla Rae added. "Mom's exhausted and is probably in bed already."

"I overheard Harley say something about her not getting any sleep last night."

"She didn't. She was with Mary McKendrick at the hospital."

"Is her friend sick?"

"Mary's new in town and a single mom. Her son suffered from a ruptured appendix and had an emergency appendectomy last night. Mom kept her company while the little boy was in the pediatric intensive care unit. She didn't want Mary to have to sit through the night alone."

Had anyone sat with Becky when Kayla Rae had been sick? Was Becky paying it forward now?

Or was she merely trying to provide comfort to someone else, support she hadn't received herself when Kayla Rae had been a seriously ill infant?

"Well, I'd better go," Kayla Rae said. "It's going to be a busy night."

Feeling alone and out of place, Priscilla watched her sister return to work.

Well, there was no point staying here any longer this evening.

She turned and searched the crowd for Cowboy. Where had he slipped off to?

There he was. Wolfing down a bowl of chili, talking to a pretty woman and apparently fitting in just fine.

Well, too bad. Priscilla was ready to go.

As she made her way toward the happy-go-lucky P.I. and a voluptuous bleached-blond cowgirl, he shot her a grin and introduced the woman as Monique.

Priscilla muttered the perfunctory, "How do you do?"

"Fine as frog's hair." Monique reached out an arm adorned with bangle bracelets and chains. "Pleased to meet you." The sincerity in her smile and her handshake wasn't convincing.

"I'm ready to leave," Priscilla told Cowboy.

"And go back to the bed-and-breakfast?" he asked, surprise washing away his boyish grin.

"Yes. The person I need to speak to won't be available until tomorrow."

"That's too bad. But why don't we stick around here for a while?"

"I'm not comfortable here," she told him, eager for them to get on their way. And if truth be told, eager to tear him away from the blonde who stood at his side.

Monique placed her hand on Cowboy's shoulder. "If you're not ready to go yet, why don't you give her your keys. I'm a great designated driver. I can take you wherever you need to go, whenever you say the word."

Priscilla, who prided herself on being civil, wanted to boot the woman in her backside. Of course, the strappy little sandals that matched her sundress wouldn't be as effective as a pointy-toed cowboy boot.

"Aw, come on, Prissy," Cowboy said. "You need to loosen up, let yourself go and have some fun for a change."

She didn't feel like arguing, but maybe she ought to remind him who was working for whom.

"All that self-control can't be healthy," he told her.

The self-control he was complaining about had seen her through a lonely childhood, her father's illness and his death. And it had carried her through the awful realization that her life had been a lie.

Her lip quivered and a tear rolled down her cheek.

Seeing Priscilla buckle nearly did Cowboy in. "Aw, dammit, Prissy. Don't do that."

She swiped at the tear streaming down her cheek, but another took its place.

Cowboy turned to Monique. "I'm afraid you're going to have to excuse us." Then he took Prissy by the hand.

She might have thought he was going outside, but he led her to the dance floor instead.

"What are you doing?"

"Trying to make you feel better."

"How do you plan to do that?"

"I'm going to show you how to have a little fun. And I'm going to start by teaching you how to do the Texas two-step."

The band, which had started playing a couple of songs ago, was in the midst of a lively tune.

"I'm not used to this kind of music."

"Trust me," he said. "If you'll just let yourself go, you'll do fine."

Hell, that philosophy had always worked for him.

But the song ended before the lesson could start.

Priscilla started to walk off the dance floor, but Cowboy grabbed her by the hand and pulled her back. "Hang tight. The next one has our names on it."

But when the band struck the first chords, Cowboy knew he was in big trouble.

It was an old Patsy Cline classic, the kind of song that drew lovers out of the privacy of a darkened booth and onto the dance floor.

But there was no way to bow out gracefully now, not when he'd made such a big deal out of dancing. So he lifted his arms, and she stepped into his embrace.

Her scent, something floral, blended with his woodsy cologne and a splash of pheromones. And the result was as magical as an enchanted forest.

As they swayed to the slow, sensual beat, his breath mingled with hers and their hearts beat in time.

He stood nearly a foot taller than her, but their bodies fit together in a complementary way—soft and hard, gentle and strong.

Despite his resolve to keep his distance, to remember that their relationship was strictly business, to realize they were smack-dab in the middle of a very public place, he couldn't help but hold her close, draw her flush against him.

Desire shot clear to his core, and his better judgment slipped by the wayside.

He released his hold just long enough to brush her hair aside, to catch her gaze with his.

Passion darkened the blue of her eyes, telling him she was feeling it, too. The heat. The rush.

There'd be hell to pay later, but he didn't care. Not now. Not while he had a demanding urge to kiss her again.

Cowboy wasn't sure who made the first move. Maybe him. Maybe her. All he knew was that he needed to taste her again, to feel the blood pounding out his need.

Her lips parted, and his tongue sought hers, dipping and tasting, mating within the warm, wet confines of her mouth.

She whimpered, yet held on tight.

He'd be damned if he knew what to do with the fire that burned inside them, but letting go didn't seem to be an option—not until another couple bumped against them, causing him to remember where they were, what they were doing.

He slowly and reluctantly broke off the kiss.

"I'm…uh…sorry about that."

"Me, too," she said, her eyes darting this way and that, her cheeks flushed. "We made a spectacle of ourselves."

Wasn't that just like Prissy? To worry about what people would think?

Hell, Cowboy had made a spectacle of himself in a bar or tavern more than once. So he wasn't the least bit sorry about that.

He was more concerned about what would have happened if they hadn't had an audience.

After that embarrassing scene on the dance floor, Cowboy had changed his mind about leaving and had driven Priscilla home.

She'd been afraid to mention the kiss or the sexual attraction that had been building. And apparently he must have felt the same way, because they had ridden back to the B and B in silence and retired to their respective rooms.

Over breakfast, they'd agreed to return to the bar in the middle of the day so Priscilla could talk to Becky while the place was relatively empty.

They arrived at the Lone Oak after lunch.

"Things are a lot quieter today," Priscilla said as they entered.

Other than two older men sitting in a corner booth, the place was nearly empty.

"Come on," Cowboy said. "We'll sit at the bar."

As they each took a stool, Harley, the heavyset bartender with a full head of salt-and-pepper hair, addressed them. "Howdy. What'll it be?"

"I'll have a Corona," Cowboy said.

Priscilla searched the nearly empty room, looking

for her mother or sister and finding neither of them. Then she blew out a sigh. To be honest, she was a little apprehensive and thought that a drink might take the edge off her nervousness. But she wanted something light that wouldn't make her lose her head. "I'll have a spritzer."

"What's that?" Cowboy asked.

"It's white wine and club soda. It's practically harmless. But don't worry. I'm not going to munch on anything salty."

"Good idea."

Moments later Harley brought them their drinks.

"Have you worked here long?" Cowboy asked the bartender.

Priscilla assumed Cowboy was going into undercover-P.I. mode and was looking for more information from the big man behind the bar.

"About two months," Harley said.

"You from around here?"

"Nope."

Priscilla suspected that the stoic bartender would prove to be a harder nut to crack than Hildy had been. But before Cowboy could ask another question, Kayla Rae entered the room.

"Hey," she said. "Welcome back."

"Hi," Priscilla said. "Is your mom available now?"

"Sure." Kayla Rae nodded toward the kitchen. "I'll go get her."

Moments later Becky walked out, wiping her

hands on a dish towel. "My daughter said you were looking for me."

Priscilla cleared her voice, hoping the words came out clear and steady. "Yes, I am. Do you have a minute?"

"Certainly."

Priscilla looked at Cowboy for support, for strength, for something. And he nodded, silently telling her to get it over with, to lay it on the line.

Harley's head was bowed over a tray that held olives, lemon slices, maraschino cherries and other cocktail garnishes, but she suspected he was listening. And so was Kayla Rae.

"Do you mind if we talk outside?" Priscilla asked. "In private?"

If Becky had been surprised by the request, she didn't show it. Instead, she folded the dish towel and placed it on the bar. "Come on."

Priscilla slid off the stool, then followed her mother across the scuffed hardwood floor to the kitchen, a small but clean room with a big grill and an industrial-size refrigerator. They proceeded through the back door and down two wooden steps.

They walked past a dented gray trash bin and a beat-up, faded red Toyota pickup that sported an empty gun rack in the rear window.

Just ahead, in the middle of a large expanse of grass that needed to be mowed, rested two mobile homes—a green-and-white, double-wide and a smaller powder-blue model. A flock of sparrows rested on an old-fashioned clothesline that stretched between them.

Whitey, the stray dog, had staked a claim under the sparse shade of a sapling that had been planted at the edge of the yard.

For a moment Priscilla wondered if her mother was going to suggest they go inside to chat.

But Becky's feet slowed, and she slid her fingers in the rear pockets of her jeans. "Are you looking for work?"

"Excuse me?" Priscilla asked.

"A job," Becky said. "I assumed that's why you wanted to talk in private."

"No." Priscilla glanced at the ground, then back to her mother's eyes. "I…"

"There's no shame in needing a handout," Becky said. "I've been there myself."

"It's not that. It's…" A breeze kicked up, blowing Priscilla's hair. "God, I don't know how to say this, but…"

"But what?"

A small voice that sounded a lot like Cowboy whispered in her head. *What are you afraid of? Just spit it out.*

Okay. She took a deep breath, then slowly released it. "Did you give birth to a daughter named Priscilla nearly twenty-five years ago?"

The woman's smile faded and she paled. Her gaze flitted between Priscilla's face and her hair. "Yes. Why do you ask?"

Had she spotted a resemblance between the child she'd lost and the woman Priscilla had become? If so, it would make this a whole lot easier.

"It's just that…" Priscilla cleared her throat again. "I think you're my mother."

"Oh, my God." Becky lifted her arms as though wanting to wrap Priscilla in a great big bear hug, then dropped them as though struggling with what she was feeling and the right thing to do. "I can't believe it. Is it really you?"

"I don't know for sure. But after my father died, I began to realize he'd been hiding a dark secret. So I hired a private investigator, and here I am."

"Your father's dead?" Becky asked.

Priscilla nodded. "Yes, two weeks ago. Liver cancer. After the funeral, I went through his old cedar chest."

Becky arched a brow. "What did it look like?"

"It wasn't anything fancy." She used her hands to show the size. "He told me he'd made it when he was in high school."

"Cliff gave it to me when we were dating. But after we split up, he insisted on taking it back. He said there was no point in me having anything he'd created. That I didn't need a hope chest when there was no hope left in our relationship."

Apparently he'd had the same philosophy when he'd taken his daughter from her bed that night.

Priscilla cleared her throat and continued. "Inside the chest I found his Army discharge papers, which said his real name was Clifford Richard Epperson. I'd always thought his name was Clinton Richards."

A million expressions shifted across Becky's face. Anger and disbelief were the most prominent.

"Apparently he had a phony birth certificate made for me," Priscilla added. "It said my mother's name was Jezzie Richards."

"Oh, for crying out loud. He always did have a lousy sense of humor. Jezzie is short for Jezebel, which is what he used to call me after I got pregnant with Kayla Rae. What a snake." Anger settled upon her mother's brow, and then she blew out a weary sigh. "I'm sorry, Priscilla. He loved you and was probably very good to you. I'm sure you cared for him. But what he did was wrong. And it was cruel."

"I know." Priscilla reached for her purse and pulled out the Polaroid photograph she'd found. "Under a lining made of wallpaper, I found this picture."

Becky took it.

Out here, in the light of day, Priscilla could spot the resemblance. Becky had filled out some and matured. But if there'd been any doubt before, there wasn't any longer.

Rebecca Mae Posey Epperson had been the young girl in the photograph.

Her mother studied the image for a moment longer, then turned to Priscilla and cupped her face with a work-roughened hand. "Honey, you have no idea how badly I've missed you, how badly I worried."

"I can imagine," Priscilla admitted. "I'm so sorry about what he did."

Becky wrapped her arms around Priscilla and pulled her into a warm, vanilla-scented embrace.

"It's been so long," her mother said, holding her close, stroking her back. "So very long."

It had been.

Priscilla closed her eyes and rested her head against her mother's cheek.

There was a lot to catch up on, but right now she didn't want to do anything but savor a maternal embrace for the first time in over twenty years.

Cowboy would just have to order another drink and wait.

Chapter Nine

While Prissy and her mother were outside, Cowboy sat at the bar and nursed his beer. The longer the women talked, the better off he'd be.

It meant they were getting things worked out. The past cleared up and the future settled. And that meant his job was done.

The sooner he could hightail it back to Manhattan, the sooner he could break free of the unwelcome attraction he felt for his client.

The kiss he and Prissy had shared on the dance floor last night had been too damn hot, too arousing for comfort.

Harley, who appeared to be checking his inventory, grunted, then addressed Cowboy. "I have to go downstairs to the stockroom. Do you need anything before I go?"

"Nope. I'm fine."

The big, quiet-spoken man nodded and went about his business, leaving Cowboy to himself.

But the silence didn't last long.

The front door swung open, and the towheaded kid Becky considered her son came tearing into the bar, a loose shoelace flipping and flopping on the floor. The white dog followed him inside, its steps slow and sure.

"Where is everyone?" Tyler asked.

"Your mom is out back, talking to…someone. Harley's in the storeroom. And I don't know where Kayla Rae is."

The little boy nodded, then reached down and rubbed Whitey's ear. When he looked up, he studied Cowboy for a moment. "Who are you?"

"Folks call me Cowboy."

"Are you?" the kid asked.

"Am I what?"

"A cowboy."

"Not really." Although he could ride a horse as well as most, he supposed.

Footsteps sounded, and Harley reentered the room, grunting under the weight of a full keg. His gaze landed on Whitey. "What's that dog doing in here?"

"Oh," the kid said. "Sorry. I forgot." But he made no move to correct the situation.

Harley placed the keg on the countertop inside the bar. "Your mom's going to be mad."

Cowboy wondered if the boy would heed the unspoken advice, but he just stood there.

Interestingly enough, Harley didn't make a big deal about it and returned to the stockroom. He was, Cowboy decided, a man of few words and—most likely—heavy thoughts.

The boy drew near. When he stopped, Whitey sat on his haunches, panting as though the effort had taxed him something fierce. When it came to thinking about that dog fathering puppies, Cowboy had to agree with Harley. The mutt just didn't seem to have the energy.

"Nice dog you have there," Cowboy said.

"Yeah. He's my best friend. And before those puppies were born, he and I were the only boys in the family."

Growing up, Cowboy could have used a dog, he supposed. By the time he'd come along, his siblings had been practically grown and gone.

Tyler kicked his tennis shoe at the hardwood floor, his brow furrowed, his lips quirked in a frown.

"What's the matter?" Cowboy asked, realizing he'd worn plenty of those expressions when he was a kid.

"Nothin'."

That had been his own stock answer whenever his mother had quizzed him. So maybe he shouldn't pry.

"Are you a dad?" the boy asked.

"Nope," Cowboy said. "Are you?"

"Heck, no. I'm just a kid."

Yeah. A kid with a canyon-size chip on his shoulder.

"Do you *have* a dad?" Tyler asked.

What was with this line of questioning? Normally Cowboy avoided talk about the past, but there was something about Tyler that reminded Cowboy of himself as a boy. And it only seemed fair to respond truthfully. "I had a father, but he died when I was about your age."

"I don't have one either," the boy said. "It sucks, huh?"

Yeah, it did.

Cowboy, who'd been called TJ back then, had been nine when his father had passed away. And even though their paths had only crossed a couple of times a week, he'd grieved for the one person who'd seemed to understand him, who'd found pleasure in his antics.

As the weeks had dragged into months, no one had seemed to care about TJ's loss or his struggle to find a place in a family that was too busy to be bothered with a mischievous little boy who just wanted to be noticed—and loved.

"Did you ever get invited to go with other kids and their dads to do stuff?" Tyler asked.

"Yeah." All the time. A father-son camping trip came to mind, as did several baseball games and Sports Day down at the YMCA.

TJ used to tell people he didn't give a rip about

sleeping outdoors or baseball. But that hadn't been the case.

"There's this big father-son thing going on at the lake tomorrow." Tyler's stance and expression were rigid, but he hadn't masked the sadness in the tone of his voice. "But I'm not going."

"Maybe you can ask someone else to go with you," Cowboy said, offering the kind of advice his mother used to dole out. The kind of advice he always rejected on principle.

What do you want me to do? he'd asked her one time. *Call 1-800-Rent-a-Dad?*

"Nah, I'm not going to do that." Tyler kicked at the floor with the toe of his worn tennis shoe. "Mom said I ought to ask Harley to go with me, but I don't want to. He's too grumpy. And I don't think he likes me."

Cowboy's heart went out to the kid. "So what's going on at the lake?"

"It's Tom Sawyer Day. They're going to fish and have a big raft race. That sort of stuff."

"Sounds fun. Think they'd let you bring a friend instead?"

Tyler shrugged, then dropped to his knees beside Whitey and nuzzled his face in the dog's fur.

Cowboy knew how it felt to be the only kid at school whose dad, even when he was alive, had been too busy to come to a Father's Day function.

"I'm pretty good at fishing," Cowboy added, wondering what in the hell he was saying, what he was about to offer.

Was he crazy? He didn't know squat about kids, especially kids who were hurting.

Or did he?

Maybe that was his expertise.

"Tom Sawyer Day sounds like the kind of thing I'd really enjoy, but I'm without a son. And since you're without a father, maybe we could...you know...team up?"

Tyler's mouth dropped in awe and his eyes brightened. "You mean you'd go with me?"

"Sure, if it's okay with your mom."

"That's really sweet," Kayla Rae said from the kitchen doorway.

Cowboy shrugged off the compliment. "It's no big deal. I like to fish."

"Still," Kayla Rae said, "it's nice of you to offer to take Tyler. Mom and I will be there, too, but he didn't want to go with girls." Then she looked at Whitey. "Uh-oh. You'd better get him out of here before Mom sees him, Tyler. You know what she said about the health department and having a dog in the bar."

Tyler scratched the top of his best friend's head. "Come on, Whitey. Let's go."

As the boy started to walk away, he turned back and shot Cowboy a grin that could turn a hardened heart to mush. "Thanks."

"No problem. We'll talk about it later, all right?"

"Okay." Tyler shot him one last grin, then dashed out the door with Whitey plodding behind.

"And speaking of my mom," Kayla Rae said, "where is she?"

"Still talking to Priscilla."

"Priscilla?"

He hadn't realized they'd never introduced themselves. But Hildy had been right about Kayla Rae being sharp.

"Oh, my God." Realization splashed across her pretty face as she had a lightbulb moment. "Is she my sister?"

"I suspect that's what she and your mom are trying to decide."

They both glanced toward the kitchen.

How much longer would Becky and Prissy stay outside?

Becky slowly released Priscilla. "I'll never forgive Cliff for taking you away—especially if he treated you badly."

"He loved me and was a good father."

"That's a relief." Becky blew out a sigh, her breath fanning a curl across her forehead. "I made a mistake getting involved with your father. But I survived and became stronger because of it."

"Did you love him?" Priscilla asked.

"I thought I did. At first. But after we were married, he became another person. And when we purchased the Lone Oak, the changes only got worse." Her mother glanced up at the sky, at a cottony cloud formation.

"What caused him to change?" Priscilla asked, wanting to make sense of it all.

"Who knows? He was raised in a loving home, although his parents were very religious and conservative. After graduation, he ran off and joined the Army. And from what I understand, he did very well. I think he actually welcomed the order and discipline. But when he was discharged, he couldn't seem to handle the freedom."

"I guess injuring his leg and getting the medical discharge was a real bummer for him," Priscilla said, remembering how her father had explained his limp.

"Is that what he told you?" her mother asked. "What a crock of bull. He'd already gotten out of the Army. But then again, he lied to me about it, too—at first. He told me he got hurt when he tried to stop a drunken brawl."

"What really happened?"

"He got involved with a married woman. And when her husband came home and found them together, he threatened to kill Cliff. So when Cliff tried to jump out a two-story window and escape, he broke his ankle, and it never healed right."

"Why didn't he go to the doctor?"

"The jealous husband was the only doctor in town back then." Her mother smiled wryly and shook her head. The she reached up and caressed a strand of Priscilla's hair. "But tell me about you. Has your life been good?"

Prior to learning about her father's selfish act and

his deception, she might have said she'd had a happy childhood. But the truth was she'd been lonely. And she'd been way too sheltered. But she didn't think her mother needed anything else to hold against her father, so she decided to soften the truth.

"I grew up in Iowa and did well in school. In fact, I received a scholarship to Brown University in Rhode Island and received a master's degree in literary arts. I'm now working as an editor for a small company that publishes children's books."

"Where do you live?" her mom asked.

"In Brooklyn, but I spend as much time as I can in Manhattan."

"Imagine that," her mom said.

"I love the city life," Priscilla quickly added. There was no reason for her mother to get her hopes up and think she'd move to Cotton Creek, although a visit now and then would be nice.

"It will take us some time to get reacquainted," Becky said. "Why don't we start by introducing you to your sister?"

"Good idea."

As they strode toward the back door of the Lone Oak, Priscilla thought about how disappointing her father had proven to be, and how cruel his selfishness had been.

She wondered if she'd ever be able to look a man in the face without wondering if he had secrets. If he'd put his own selfish desire ahead of a woman he cared about.

They walked through the kitchen and back into the bar, where Kayla Rae waited with Cowboy.

His gaze met hers, and something unspoken passed between them. An understanding that all was well.

He flashed her that familiar, heart-spinning grin that spoke of his happiness, his support. His relief that things had worked out for her.

Cowboy was proving to be a good friend. What a wonderful man he was. The kind a woman wanted in her corner, the kind she could lean on when life took an unexpected turn.

And the fact that he packed a dynamite kiss suggested he would make an even better lover.

The next morning, after breakfast at the B and B, Cowboy drove Priscilla to the Lone Oak, where he left her to ride in the car with her mother and sister, then he and Tyler followed them to Larkspur Lake.

Becky had gone all out fixing a picnic lunch that was big enough for the entire town. By her enthusiasm, it was obvious that she appreciated Cowboy stepping in and taking the boy to the father-son event.

"I'm looking forward to having a fish fry tonight," she told them in the parking lot at the lake, before wishing them good luck and sending them on their way.

But so far the only things biting were the mosquitoes.

Cowboy slapped at another one.

"How come we haven't caught anything yet?"

Tyler asked. "It's going to be hard to win the biggest fish contest if we don't even get a single bite."

"Don't worry about that. There's always the raft race. And besides, half the fun is being out here, don't you think?"

"Yeah," Tyler said. "I love my mom and Kayla Rae, but it's nice being out here with another guy, huh?"

"Real nice." Cowboy ruffled the boy's head. And being outdoors on a day like this was even better.

The sun was warm, yet a breeze had kicked up. Cowboy wasn't one to talk to God, let alone try and strike a bargain. But he figured there was no harm in asking for a favor for someone else.

I know You're probably too busy to be bothered by a little boy fishing, but do You think You could spare a trout or a bass? I'm not asking for Tyler to come out a winner. Shoot, he'd be happy with something old and on its last fin.

"My mom said you were a private investigator," Tyler said.

"Yep. That's right."

"And that you helped Priscilla find us."

Cowboy nodded, then slapped at his neck and decided to tack a P.S. onto his silent request. *And if it's not too much trouble, could you send these pesky critters to the other side of the lake?*

Tyler shifted his weight to one foot. "How much does it cost to find someone?"

"That all depends. Some folks are harder to find than others."

"What about a dad who went to Boise?"

Cowboy glanced down at the boy, saw sincerity and sadness in those big blue eyes. "I thought you said your father died."

"No. You said yours died. I just told you that I didn't have one anymore. But I guess he could have died. I don't know."

Cowboy wasn't sure what to say. "When did you last see him?"

"When I was seven. He was supposed to start a new job and get us a house to live in. He left me with... Well, Becky isn't really my mom, but since I never had one and she never had a little boy, she wanted to be mine."

"So your dad left you with her?"

"Uh-huh. He was supposed to come and get me in a month or two. But he never did."

Cowboy didn't know what to say. And there was no one around to ask or to pass the kid off to. So he was on his own.

And struggling, mind you.

"Hey!" Tyler held tight to a pole that bent at the tip. "I got a bite."

"You sure did," Cowboy said, ready to move on to a happier subject.

After a respectable tug-of-war between boy and fish, Cowboy helped Tyler reel in a whopper.

Maybe the Old Boy Upstairs cared about little boys after all.

A whistle blew and a voice came over a bullhorn.

"Time's up! Bring your catch down to the scale so we can choose the winners. And after that we'll go down to the boat launch and board the rafts."

"Boy, just in the nick of time," Tyler said as he eyed the big trout that had a fair chance of taking first place.

As they packed the remnants of a killer fried-chicken lunch back in the cooler, Cowboy made a mental note to ask Becky about Tyler's dad.

He wondered if she'd filed a missing-persons report or whether the guy had just left his son in Cotton Creek without a backward glance.

Some guys did that. And frankly, Cowboy thought those who did weren't much better than pond scum.

He had no intention of ever getting married and having a family. But if he ever were responsible for putting a child on the earth, he wouldn't desert the kid.

"Are you going to live in Cotton Creek?" Tyler asked.

"Nope. I've got to go back to work in New York."

"But you'll come back to Texas for a visit, won't you?" the boy asked, eyes hopeful.

Cowboy didn't want to lie to the kid, but he didn't want him getting false hopes either. "I'll be in Dallas next weekend."

"Cool," Tyler said. "Then maybe you'll come back to Cotton Creek someday, too."

"Who knows," Cowboy said, even though it wasn't likely.

Then he turned his attention heavenward, hoping that the Old Boy was still listening and he could tack on another P.S. to his prayer.

Because this request was bigger than the first one had been.

You know as well as I do that this kid needs someone he can depend on, God. Don't let him latch on to me.

The poor kid has already had more than his share of disappointment in life.

Chapter Ten

Tyler received a gold trophy for snagging the biggest catch of the day and a fourth-place ribbon for his and Cowboy's efforts in the raft race.

They would have made a clean sweep if Tyler hadn't lost his balance and fallen into the lake when they were three-quarters of the way across. Cowboy didn't know if the kid could swim or not, so he'd jumped in after him. And by the time they'd gotten back on the raft, a couple of other teams had shot past them.

But what the heck. It had been good for a few laughs, especially for the three women who'd been cheering them on from the bank.

Later that afternoon, after they'd returned to the

Lone Oak, Becky fried that single trout into a huge platter that served two hungry fishermen, a bartender, her daughters and herself, with fish to spare—at least that's how it appeared.

If Tyler had realized his respectable-size trout hadn't been that big, he didn't say.

But Cowboy figured Becky must have stopped by the market on the way home and picked up more fish—not all of it trout. Otherwise, he'd been a witness to a miracle of biblical proportions.

What she'd done had been pretty cool. Not every mom would go to that length to make her son feel proud.

Once they'd eaten their fill, Cowboy decided to go back to the bed-and-breakfast for a shower. Prissy seemed to be doing a good job bonding with her family, so he left her at the Lone Oak, headed out the door and into the parking lot.

As he climbed into the Expedition, Becky stepped out of the bar and approached him.

"I can't begin to tell you how much I appreciate what you've done for us. First in helping Priscilla find me and then taking Tyler to Tom Sawyer Day. He had a wonderful time. We all did."

"No problem," Cowboy said as he closed the driver's door. "But tell me something about Tyler's father."

"His name is Frank Markham. And he asked me to look after his son more than a year ago."

"What do you know about him?"

"Only that he's a nice guy—when he isn't drinking. And he's also got a serious gambling problem. A couple of months before he left, he got in over his head with a bookie and sold his house to pay his debt. He and Tyler lived in their car for a while. Then an old friend from Idaho offered him a job working construction, and he was hoping to get his life back on track by moving to Boise. But he didn't want to drag Tyler there until he got settled."

"Did he ever call or write?"

"No. And he promised to." The breeze kicked a strand of hair onto Becky's cheek, and she brushed it aside. "After a year and not even a phone call, I have this awful feeling that he won't be coming back. And I think Tyler senses it, too."

Cowboy nodded in agreement. "I hope you don't mind, but I'd like to look for him."

"That's great. But I've had some unexpected expenses and don't have a lot to spare right now. I might be able to handle a couple of days' work."

"I'm not going to charge you," Cowboy said. "I'm doing it as a favor to Tyler."

Relief flooded her face. "Thanks. I appreciate that."

"Let's not mention anything to Tyler yet," he said. "We can decide what to tell him if I uncover anything."

"I'm afraid you're going to find that Frank has either had an accident or met with foul play. He might have had some serious personal problems, but he loved Tyler and wouldn't have deserted him."

Cowboy rested his left wrist on top of the steering

wheel, yet didn't turn on the ignition. "What will happen to the boy if his father is dead?"

"Before he left, Frank gave me temporary custody. But over the past year I've come to love that little boy as if he were my own, and nothing would make me happier than to adopt him."

That's all Cowboy needed to know. He'd feel like a real jerk if he uncovered anything that might make the kid's life worse.

"Thanks again," Becky said.

"My pleasure." Then he turned on the engine, backed out of the drive and headed for the B and B. On the way, he snatched his cell phone and gave Rico a call.

His boss answered on the second ring.

"My job is wrapping up here," Cowboy told him. "But unless you've got something pressing for me to do, I'd like to stick around for a couple more days."

"Weren't you going to Dallas next weekend?" Rico asked.

"Yeah." His mother wasn't one to cancel dinner parties, especially one that was going to launch her only son-in-law's campaign for congressman.

"What we've got here can wait," Rico said. "Go ahead and take next week off."

"Thanks." Cowboy wasn't sure he needed that much time, but he could use a couple of days to himself.

"Listen," Rico said, "I'd better go. Molly and I are

having my mom and her husband over for dinner, and I forgot to pick up the salad fixings. By the time I stop by the market, I'm going to be late getting home."

"How is that pretty little wife of yours?" Cowboy asked.

"Molly's doing great. And so am I. Believe it or not, I love being married."

"You're still in the honeymoon stage," Cowboy reminded him. But the truth was he'd seen the way Rico and his bride looked at each other and he had a feeling the romance wasn't likely to end any time soon.

A relationship like that had to be one in a million.

"I'm going to do my best to keep the honeymoon going for a very long time," Rico said, his voice taking on what could only be described as a starry-eyed tone.

Cowboy shook his head and clucked his tongue. "Sounds like you've got it bad."

"Hey, pal, you should be so lucky to have it this bad."

Then they said goodbye and disconnected the line.

Cowboy couldn't see himself married. On a whim, he tried to conjure up a vision of his life if he ever suffered a lapse in judgment and got hitched.

Without any prompting, a certain prim redhead took center stage—a woman who was *so* not his type.

But in his mind he saw Prissy puttering around the kitchen wearing a dress and a string of pearls that would make June Cleaver smile.

Then the image faded and a new one appeared.

Prissy in the bedroom wearing a Garfield nightshirt that was about as sexy as a flannel gown. But as she slipped out of the nightie, revealing a pair of skimpy white panties and a lacy bra...

Damn. He was going to have to do something about those mental pop-ups. And the unwelcome sexual attraction that seemed to be growing by leaps and bounds.

If there was anything he didn't need, it was a woman who would turn up her nose at some down-home fun.

Of course, she was just a client, he reminded himself. A soon-to-be *former* client. He had to cut bait and run before he got in any deeper.

Thank God she wasn't his lover.

Okay, so they'd shared a couple of hot let's-get-naked kisses. But that wasn't the same thing.

He just hoped Prissy wouldn't think it was.

After a shower and a change of clothes, Cowboy decided to check out of his room at the B and B. Hildy had been surprised, but she had plenty of new guests to dote on—a retired couple from northern California and a budding romance novelist wanting to get a feel for what it was like living in a small town in Texas.

Cowboy hadn't really wanted to stay at the

Stardust Inn, the place he'd referred to as a "no-tell motel" when they'd driven into town. But it wasn't so bad. And his options were limited if he was going to stick around for another day or so.

The motel didn't look like much on the outside, but the inside was clean, the bed was comfortable and the TV reception was good.

So now that he'd showered—he hadn't seen a need to shave—he swaggered back into the Lone Oak, intending to put thoughts of Prissy behind him and have some fun.

Of course, somewhere along the way he needed to tell her he was leaving and she'd have to fend for herself.

Not only was he doing them both a favor, emotionally speaking, but he was also saving her money, since she no longer had to pay his expenses.

It was all for the best.

Inside the Lone Oak, people were laughing and mingling, but Cowboy bellied up to the bar. Yet this time, instead of nursing a beer or two all night, he ordered a scotch with a splash of water.

He hadn't quite finished it when an attractive blonde entered the front door and quickly scanned the place. He wasn't sure if she was looking for someone in particular or whether anyone would do.

No one else seemed to have noticed her, even though a woman like her was hard to miss.

She wasn't what he'd call pretty, but she had a great shape and knew how to enhance it. That pair of denim shorts she was wearing would barely cover her butt if she bent over. And her snug red T-shirt showed off every voluptuous curve.

If truth be told, she was the kind of woman Cowboy gravitated to on a night that started off with scotch.

And she was just the kind of woman who would get his mind off a prissy little redhead who wasn't his type—a woman who'd snaked her way into his subconscious, suggesting some sort of commitment was in order.

A commitment Cowboy had no intention of making.

The blonde seemed to zero in on him, then joined him at the bar and reached out a hand. Her acrylic nails had been squared off and fashioned to look like a perfect French manicure. "Hi, there. My name's Twyla."

"Folks call me Cowboy," he said, preferring— as he always did—to introduce himself with a nickname. It was a great way to detach himself from the Whittakers and to maintain his privacy while projecting himself as a what-you-see-is-what-you-get sort of guy.

Twyla smiled, revealing a chipped front tooth, the only bodily imperfection he'd spotted so far.

She took the bar stool next to his. "Can I buy you a drink, Cowboy?"

"Sure," he said, sliding her a charming grin. "I like a woman who knows how to have a good time."

"Well, what do you know? You sure pegged me

right. I'm an expert when it comes to having fun."
Twyla leaned forward, her breasts pressing against
the bar and straining the fabric of her shirt. "Yoo hoo,
Harley. Will you open up a tab for me and get us a
couple of tequila shooters?"

Yep. Twyla was a girl who knew how to party.

"Do you come here often?" Cowboy asked her.

"I *come*…every chance I get."

He imagined she did, and tossed her a carefree
grin. Yet even through the alcohol-induced buzz, his
conscience tweaked, and a real push-pull kicked into
play.

Flirting with Twyla while being with Priscilla
was doing a real number on him. Not that he was
actually *with* Priscilla.

So why did it feel as if he was?

They'd only kissed a couple of times.

Hell, he was a player, not a man who wanted to
settle down. And he damn sure wasn't the kind of
guy Prissy needed. So why let her get the wrong
idea about him?

Women like Twyla, on the other hand, weren't
looking for a relationship and were usually just as
happy as he was to remain unencumbered.

That's why he never dated women looking to
settle down. Women who expected more out of him
than he could provide.

Twyla called to Harley again. When the bartender
caught her eye, she lifted her index finger and circled
it, silently requesting another round.

Harley nodded, understanding what she wanted, and went to work placing her order.

In the meantime, Twyla ran her hand along Cowboy's forearm in a let's-ditch-this-place sort of way.

Her touch and silent invitation should have spiked his pulse, but it didn't.

So where was that sexual rush he ought to be feeling? That urge to pay his tab and ask her whether they should go to his place or hers?

Instead he fought the compulsion to turn around, to look for Prissy. To make some kind of excuse.

Damn. Where had the guilt come from?

When Harley placed the second round of shooters in front of them, Cowboy took the small glass in hand. But for some dumb reason, he looked over his shoulder.

And caught Prissy watching him.

Priscilla had half a notion to stomp over to the bar and make a scene. But what good would that do?

She and Cowboy weren't a couple. And she didn't have any right to demand anything from him.

Still, when he turned back around and focused his attention on that bleached blonde, her chest ached. It hurt to see him with a woman who didn't seem to mind if she looked cheap and easy.

"Leave it to Twyla to zero in on a good-looking stranger," Kayla Rae said. "She's already run through most of the willing men in Cotton Creek."

Priscilla rubbed her palms along her hips and thighs, her fingers itching to curl into fists.

"Are you going to just sit here and watch it all happen?" Kayla asked.

"What else can I do? It's not as though we're dating or anything."

"The heck it isn't," her sister said, showing a flash of Latin spunk. "I saw you two swapping tongues on the dance floor last night. And you might not have any kind of formal commitment, but he owes you more respect than that. I'd at least go over there and throw your soda pop in his face."

Priscilla's lips quirked into a smile, even though her heart was beating in a dull thud in her chest. "That wouldn't solve anything."

"No, but it might make you feel a lot better."

Priscilla wasn't so sure about that. She watched Twyla place a hand on Cowboy's shoulder and whisper in his ear. Watched him chuckle at whatever she'd said.

"Uh-oh," her sister said. "You're in love with him, aren't you."

It wasn't really a question, which was a good thing, since Priscilla really didn't have an answer. She didn't love Cowboy. But she feared it was more than attraction buzzing around her heart.

"Have you told him?" her sister asked.

"Told him what?"

"How you feel."

"I don't even know what I'm feeling—other than

a growing desire to grab him by the front of his shirt and shake some sense into him."

"You don't need to get violent," Kayla Rae said. "But sometimes a woman has to go after what she wants. And men aren't mind readers."

"Okay. So I'm attracted to him. He's a wonderful man. He's been so helpful, so supportive. And if it's not love that I'm feeling, it could develop over time." Priscilla blew out a sigh. "But what if he's not interested in me?"

"If you aren't willing to risk it all for a man, then he's not worth having."

Cowboy glanced over his shoulder again, and their gazes met. Maybe he was feeling something for her, too. Maybe he was just being polite to Twyla.

Priscilla tried to imagine what her friend Sylvia would advise if she were here. And that wasn't hard to do.

On the night Sylvia had given Priscilla Cowboy's business card, she'd made her opinion on the subject pretty clear.

God knows your love life could sure use a shot in the tush. And believe me, Pris, this guy will do it. If I weren't involved with Warren, I'd have jumped his bones in a heartbeat.

And if truth be told, Prissy had to agree with her friend as well as her sister.

"You're right, Kayla. Maybe I should give it a try." But she remained rooted to the floor.

"Well, don't just stand here and do nothing,"

Kayla said. "Either raise a ruckus or tell Cowboy that if he's looking to score tonight, it might as well be with you."

She made it sound so easy.

Was it?

"I'm probably going to hate myself in the morning," Prissy said.

"Twyla could seduce a snake," Kayla Rae said. "And if you let that poor, unsuspecting guy fall for her line of bull, you're going to feel like crap tomorrow anyway."

Her sister had a point.

As Priscilla started across the barroom floor, she hoped she wasn't making the biggest mistake of her life.

When she reached Cowboy's side, she placed a hand on his shoulder and gave it a gentle squeeze. "Hi."

He turned his head and their eyes met. A sheepish expression suggested he wasn't nearly as footloose as he claimed to be.

Her heart beat erratically, and she hoped her nervousness didn't spill into her voice. "Having fun?"

Not really, Cowboy wanted to say. He'd never felt so unbalanced in his life. And it was all Prissy's fault.

But for some dumb, inexplicable reason, he suggested that she sit down and join him and Twyla.

"Thanks." Prissy pulled out the bar stool next to him and took a seat.

"Would you like a drink?" he asked her.

"No, thanks. I've had my fill of diet cola. But on the bright side, that means I can be your designated driver tonight."

He had his limits and knew when to call a cab, but he let the subject drop. Instead, he picked up his shot glass and threw back another tequila.

It didn't sit well, and his arm slowly lowered. The party spirit he'd been trying to foster had died a sudden death. If he had another drink, it would be water.

Twyla nudged his arm, then made a mock whisper that was loud enough for Priscilla to hear. "I hope she's your sister, because I'm in the mood for love tonight, not a catfight."

Yeah, well, he'd thought he was in the mood for sex, too. But Twyla wasn't as appealing as she should be—and not just because Prissy's presence was making him feel awkward.

He'd been getting antsy before Priscilla even took a seat beside him.

"I'm not his sister," Prissy told Twyla. She took a deep breath, then let it out. "But I'd like to be his lover."

Cowboy damn near choked on his drink. She would?

Someone must have slipped something into her diet cola. She had to be high on something. Why else would the prim and proper woman come on so strong?

Not that her revelation wasn't appealing.

Or arousing.

"In that case," Twyla said, "maybe we ought to let him choose which one of us he wants."

Things were getting *way* out of hand.

"You know, ladies," Cowboy said, getting to his feet, "I think I'll make it an early night and watch a little TV in my room."

"Sounds boring," Twyla said. "Looks like I'll have to find a man who knows how to have fun and isn't afraid to make a decision."

Rather than respond, Cowboy called Harley over and closed out his tab.

Prissy slid off the bar stool, then held out her hand. "Give me the keys."

When he reached into his pocket and handed them to her, she slid him a pretty smile that broadsided his heart.

Something told him he'd just placed more than his keys in her hands.

And he wasn't that drunk.

Really.

As they left the bar, the night air had a sobering effect. And so did Prissy.

On the way to the stall where he'd parked the Expedition, she slipped her free hand in his. "I meant what I said in there."

About what? he wanted to know. But he was afraid to ask. Afraid to hear her say she wanted to be his lover all over again.

But worse than that, he was afraid that she'd

realize he'd already chosen her over the fun-loving, forward blonde the moment Twyla had sat beside him.

And that scared him spitless.

They rode in silence, but as they neared the turnoff to the B and B, he realized he hadn't told her about checking out.

"Keep going straight," he said. "Toward town."

"Why?"

"Because I checked out of the Posey house this evening and into the Stardust Inn."

His admission broadsided Priscilla, and she nearly hit the brakes. "Why did you do that?"

"I...don't know."

Yes, he did. But apparently he didn't want to tell her why.

Did it have anything to do with the kisses they'd shared, with the turn their professional relationship seemed to be taking?

The man might be sweet and sexy, but he was frustrating, too.

"Actually," Cowboy said, "I decided to move out of the B and B because I'm no longer on your case."

Again, silence permeated the inside of the Expedition.

"And because I value my privacy," he added. "It felt weird staying in a guest room of someone's home."

Prissy didn't quiz him anymore and continued to drive, but she still suspected he hadn't been honest.

That he'd been holding back something he hadn't wanted to admit.

When they reached the Stardust Inn, Cowboy pointed to the left. "It's number one-fourteen. And it's on the back side."

She followed his directions, parking the SUV in the space in front of his room.

He sat for a moment, apparently in no hurry to get out of the vehicle. Then he turned in his seat and looked over the console at her.

Their gazes met, and he reached for her cheek and cupped her jaw. His thumb grazed her skin, sending a shiver of heat through her veins.

Her heart spun out of control and her hope soared.

"Okay," he said. "I'll be honest. Kissing you wasn't in my game plan. And neither was this damned attraction I'm feeling. I'm not the kind of man you need to get involved with. And that's the real reason I moved out of the Posey house. I don't want to see you get hurt."

His words knocked the wind right out of her. He felt it, too. The attraction, the desire.

He might think he wasn't the kind of man she needed, but she knew differently.

She thought about all the times he'd reached out to her, comforted her with a touch of his hand. And she'd seen how good he was with Tyler.

No, he was wrong. There was a sweet side to him, a tender side he hid from others. And she'd seen it clearly.

She placed her hand over his, holding his fingers against her cheek, his palm against her jaw. "Invite me into your room."

A bewildered expression swept across his face, and she sensed her boldness had surprised him. To be honest, it had surprised her, too. But she meant what she'd said. She wanted to make love tonight.

With him.

"Aw, Prissy." His gaze flitted from her eyes to her lips and back again. "You don't mean that. It would be crazy. And wrong."

But instead of putting up a fight, his fingers slid to the back of her neck and he drew her mouth to his.

Chapter Eleven

The kiss started slowly and almost apologetically. But when Prissy parted her lips, offering Cowboy a sweet taste of her, he was lost in a swirl of desire.

His tongue sought hers, dipping and mating. Heat surged and his hormones soared, kicking his pulse into high gear and sending his blood racing to all the right places.

He wanted to lay her down, to stretch out against her, to let her know how badly he wanted to make love to her. But the damn console and gearshift were in the way.

Still, they continued to kiss as their hands caressed, explored. Groped.

Their breaths came out in steamy little pants, fogging the windows of the vehicle, where they made out like a couple of teenagers parked at Lover's Lane—kids who had no worries about tomorrow, no thoughts about the future.

It was crazy. Wild.

But oh-so sweet.

Cowboy tried to remind himself that Prissy was his client, but that really wasn't true any longer.

When had she become more than that?

He wasn't sure. But somewhere along the way his sexual longing for her had grown too compelling to ignore, too strong to resist.

Get a grip, his conscience said, trying to make one last-ditch effort to encourage self-control, but his erection wasn't buying it.

She'd said she wanted to make love. So who was he to argue? Not when he couldn't think of anything he wanted to do more than have sex with her.

Regret was bound to crop up later, but he'd deal with it in the morning. And if backed into an emotional corner, he'd blame it on the alcohol, even though he'd never felt so sober in his life.

Or so cramped.

His brains might be having an out-of-body experience, but his libido knew that it was stupid to remain in a vehicle when there was a bed only steps away.

"Come on," he told her. "Let's take this inside."

"Good idea."

They climbed from the SUV and headed for the door to his motel room. She waited for him to slip the key into the lock and let them in.

The yellow glow of the porch lit the inside until he could flip the switch and provide an illuminated view of the decor: a king-size bed with a simple blue plaid spread, a plain headboard with a couple of matching, nondescript pieces of bedroom furniture that hadn't been in style since the seventies—and then only in places that provided lodging for those on a limited budget.

He nearly apologized for the sparse setting, thinking she deserved the honeymoon suite in a luxurious five-star hotel. But instead he welcomed her into the only place they had available. "It's not much. But it's all I can offer you tonight."

"You won't hear me complain." The warmth and sincerity of her smile turned his conscience inside out, making him believe, if only for this moment, that the decision to make love had been their only choice.

So he took her in his arms and resumed their hungry kiss. His tongue dipped and danced inside her mouth, and when she leaned into him, a moan formed low in his throat.

He explored the gentle contours of her body, the slope of her back, the sides of her waist. Up, down and around to her breasts, where he caressed her through the fabric of her blouse and bra.

His thumbs skimmed over her stimulated nipples, and her breath caught. Then, without removing her mouth from his, she began to unbutton her top. As she tugged it over her shoulders, he broke the kiss long enough to watch, to see her slip the material the rest of the way off, leaving her standing before him in a lacy pink bra and a pair of black slacks.

Something told him she wore matching pink panties as sexy and skimpy as the bra. And when she removed her pants, sliding them over her hips, he realized he'd been right.

She stepped out of the last of her clothing, then almost shyly unhooked her bra, freeing her breasts.

Her beauty overwhelmed him, and so did the fact that she was offering herself to him—no strings attached, he hoped.

Had he ever been given such a sweet gift?

As he marveled at her petite perfection, he couldn't keep his thoughts to himself. Yet his voice came out huskier than usual. Softer. "Aw, Prissy. You're beautiful."

He removed his shirt and tossed it on the floor, wanting desperately to feel her skin on his, her breasts splayed against his chest.

She unleashed his belt, then undid the top button of his jeans and reached for his zipper.

He'd never wanted a woman more—a startling fact that ought to scare the hell out of him. But he couldn't seem to focus on anything other than the driving need to slide inside her.

As she struggled with his jeans, he meant to help until a disappointing realization struck.

His hand reached for hers and froze over her fingers. "I don't suppose you thought to bring any condoms with you."

Her eyes widened. "You don't have any?"

"Not *with* me. I have some at home, but I hadn't planned on sleeping with you. I don't get involved with my clients."

What he'd told her was true. But for a guy who liked to be prepared for the unexpected, he couldn't believe he hadn't packed any in his shaving kit. Maybe to prevent himself from losing his head over Prissy, he'd subconsciously forgotten them. Of course, none of that mattered right now.

Prissy didn't respond right away, but he saw the disappointment on her face.

"That's too bad," she finally said. "Especially since I'm not a client anymore."

"Yeah. I know."

There were a variety of ways they could pleasure each other without actually risking pregnancy. Then, when the drugstore opened in the morning, they could...

Wait a second.

He brightened. "We're in luck."

"We are?"

"Yeah. But I hope you like neon-green. It's the one you gave me when we were at Riley's in Brooklyn."

He strode over to the table where he'd left his briefcase, then dug around until he found the little packet.

When he held it up and flashed her a victorious smile, she strode toward him as though she'd done this a hundred times and he was a stage-struck virgin.

She reached out. "Here. Let me."

He handed it over, then watched as she tore into the foil packet and removed the protection. And as she rolled it on, her touch nearly shot him over the edge. "You're driving me crazy, Prissy. And making me love it."

"Good."

Priscilla had never felt so bold. So in control. And not just of a sexual situation, but of her life, her future.

When she'd finished protecting them, she slipped her arms round Cowboy's neck, then kissed him until she was weak-kneed and senseless.

Apparently he knew the effect he was having on her, because he swept her into his arms and carried her to the bed, where he gently laid her down. Then he joined her, loving her with his hands and his mouth until she was wild with need.

As he hovered over her, he brushed a strand of hair from her brow. "I want to make this special, something you'll always remember."

There was no doubt about that. She was going to remember him, remember this night, when she was old and gray. When their children had children of their own.

They hadn't admitted what was happening to them, but it didn't matter. She sensed his feelings for her were every bit as strong as hers were for him.

He might not know it yet, but she was pinning her heart on him. And her trust. She knew he was nothing like her father. That he would never use her for his own selfish and vindictive reasons. And in her heart she knew he was the kind of man she could depend on through thick and thin.

"Tell me what you like, what feels good," he said. "I want to make it better for you."

"Just love me, Cowboy."

If he realized her words meant so much more than the act, he didn't say.

And even if he wasn't ready to admit what he felt for her, she offered him all she had.

As she opened for him, he eased himself deep inside her. She arched to meet him, and as he thrust in and out, she moved with him, taking and giving until they were both caught in the throes of a powerful orgasm. And all she could do was hold on tight, relishing what they'd shared.

As the last wave of pleasure ebbed, he rolled to the side, taking her with him.

There was so much she wanted to tell him, so much she wanted to hear. But that could wait until tomorrow.

Right now, she was content to lie quietly in his arms, wrapped in the warmth of his embrace.

And basking in the unspoken promise of his love.

The morning sunlight peered through a bent slat in the blinds, taunting Cowboy until he woke.

Priscilla slept in his arms, her back fitting nicely

against his chest, her bottom resting in his lap. His right arm was tucked under her head, and the other draped over her breast.

Their lovemaking had left his head spinning. And his only complaint had been not having a second condom.

Or a third. Heck, he could have used an entire box.

But just as he'd suspected, regret had dawned with the morning light.

What if Prissy expected something from him? Something permanent?

He ought to come up with some kind of excuse to leave, to take her back to the Lone Oak, where she belonged. To pretend that sex hadn't changed anything between them.

Sometimes it didn't.

But with a woman like Prissy?

She arched her back and stretched.

Now was the time to slide his arm out from under her head and roll out of bed. But for some reason, he drew her close and nuzzled her neck instead.

Why in blazes had he done that? He must be losing his grip on reality.

She slowly turned around until she was facing him. Her hair, tousled from sleep and lovemaking, looked as sexy as ever. More so, he supposed.

Her eyes, while still sleepy, glimmered with feminine satisfaction. "Hi."

"Good mornin'." He really needed to get the hell

out of Dodge, but for some reason, he continued to hold her close.

But that had to stop. He couldn't let her get the wrong idea.

He slowly withdrew his right arm and propped himself up on an elbow. "Listen, Priscilla. Last night was great, and I wouldn't mind doing it again. But I hope you're not expecting more from me than I can give. I'm not the kind of guy a woman like you needs."

Something flickered in her eyes.

Disappointment, he decided.

And pain?

Probably. But it was better to hurt her now than later, when she might think she had a vested interest in him.

"Tell me," she said, "what does a woman like me need?"

"For one thing, a man who won't bail when things get tough. And I'm not that guy."

"What makes you say that?"

"I don't do well when relationships get bogged down with emotion." That's why he kept things superficial, especially when it came to lovers.

"What are you talking about?"

He didn't know how to explain without going into more detail than he was comfortable sharing. "Let's just say that I've failed a couple of friends in the past. And I'm not eager to be in that position again. I don't mind being your temporary lover, but if you want anything more than that, I can't give it to you."

She studied him without comment. Just taking it all in, he supposed. Then she trailed her fingers along his cheek in a gentle caress. "Who did you fail?"

Aw, man. She didn't expect him to resurrect all that, did she?

His thoughts drifted to Jenny, to the teenager whose death he'd tried his damnedest to blame on his mother. But deep inside he knew whose fault it had been.

He never talked about Jenny anymore. Not since the day after her funeral, when his sister, Katie, had come home for a visit. She'd entered the den and found him teary-eyed and overwhelmed by guilt. He'd unloaded on her, though. And she'd held him while he'd cried, offering more comfort than he'd received in a long time. Comfort he didn't really deserve.

The whole experience had been embarrassing, not to mention somewhat emasculating for an adolescent who constantly tried to prove he was grown-up to four older siblings who had families of their own.

But for some reason, lying here with Prissy, he wasn't as guarded as he usually was. And hell, maybe if he leveled with her, if he gave her a couple of examples, she'd come to the realization all by herself.

When it came to emotional support, Trenton James Whittaker didn't have squat to give.

He inhaled, hoping for a whiff of courage and catching the scent of their lovemaking instead. Then he slowly blew it out.

"When I was sixteen, I started seeing the new girl in school. She was pretty, but shy. And her name was Jenny." He looked at Prissy, saw her watching him, listening.

She didn't speak, didn't prod him. So he continued, slowly but carefully, ready to roll back the memory if it became too much to deal with.

"One day, when I had the house to myself, I invited her over. We talked, then listened to music. After a while, we started kissing. It was all pretty innocent."

Prissy didn't say a word. She just sat there, letting him speak.

Okay. So far, so good.

"My mom came home unexpectedly, and even though we were fully clothed and in the living room, not in the bedroom, she flipped out." His gaze drifted to the ceiling, to the outdated popcorn coating that had yellowed over time.

"Then what happened?" Prissy asked, as though she knew she'd need to draw the tragic story out of him. As though it might be cathartic for him to reveal it all.

And maybe she was right.

"My mom, who's big on social decorum, made a big deal about us being alone in the house without a chaperone. And she called Jenny a low-class tramp, and the poor girl ran outside in tears." He cleared his throat, hoping that it would make it easier for him to open up, to share. "I was embarrassed and angry, so I lashed out at my mom, using a few words I'd never used in front of her before. Then I went after Jenny."

Prissy placed her hand on his chest, stroking the area over his heart. "That sounds like you were being pretty supportive to me."

Maybe. But when things took a heavy turn, he hadn't been able to cope.

"I followed her outside and we hung around while she cried. I told her to forget what my mother had said, not to worry about it. But then Jenny told me something I hadn't expected, something that was too heavy for me to handle."

"What did she say?"

"Her family had recently moved to town, but I hadn't realized why. About six months earlier, she'd snuck out of the house late one night to meet a boy she'd been going steady with. But before she could reach him, she was raped by a couple of strangers. She wasn't dealing with it very well, so her parents moved to a new city, hoping that it would be easier for her to leave the memories behind and move on with her life."

"I'm sure your mom's comment didn't help."

"No, it didn't. Apparently Jenny was struggling with guilt, thinking she'd brought it on herself. She also felt soiled and dirty. And because of that, my mother's words had cut her to the bone."

"How tragic."

"Yeah. And I couldn't think of anything to say or

do. So I fumbled around with apologies and telling her my mom was insensitive. But hell, I was just as bad. I couldn't walk Jenny home fast enough."

"How old were you?" she asked.

"Almost sixteen."

"And you think just because you couldn't come up with the right things to say to comfort someone who'd suffered something violent and brutal, that you failed her? This world is full of people who don't know what to say or how to help people who've been victimized. That's what trained professionals are for."

He glanced away from her understanding gaze and again looked at the ceiling, at a brown water stain in the corner.

A part of him wanted to let the conversation die, to let it go at that. But maybe Prissy ought to know it all. Then maybe she'd realize why a relationship with him wasn't in her best interests.

"That evening," he continued, "Jenny called and wanted me to come over and talk with her. Her voice sounded kind of weak and shaky, and I was afraid she was going to unload on me again. So I told her I was grounded and couldn't go anywhere for a week."

"That's when you think you failed her?"

Yeah. Jenny had needed someone to talk to, and he'd refused to listen, refused to be there for her. But he'd let Prissy come to her own conclusion.

"Two days later, at school, the rumor mill was buzzing about the new girl and how she'd committed suicide in the middle of the night." He blew out a sigh, then rolled onto his back and stared at the ceiling that really needed to be refurbished.

Prissy placed a hand on his jaw and drew his gaze back to her. "That wasn't your fault."

"No? Then why does it feel that way?"

"How was a teenager supposed to know the right thing to say or do in a situation like that? What about her parents? Hadn't they seen it coming? Hadn't they considered getting her into counseling?"

"According to what I heard, the evening she committed suicide, her younger sister had thrown a fit at the dinner table, complaining about the family move and missing the friends she'd been forced to leave behind. And after that I guess Jenny just decided that life wasn't worth the struggle."

"I would imagine you're not the only one feeling responsible," Priscilla said.

He supposed there had been a lot of guilt to go around. And like him, he imagined her parents and sister were still feeling plenty of it. But a few weeks later they moved again, and he'd never seen or heard anything about them since.

But that didn't mean he hadn't failed Jenny.

"Did you talk to anyone?" Prissy asked.

"Like a counselor?"

She nodded.

"No."

At the time, he'd felt overwhelmed and alone. And since then he'd dealt with it by not setting himself up to get into that kind of situation again. That's why he kept all his relationships light and easy.

Of course, there'd been a time when one had crept up on him unexpectedly.

"I had another chance to be someone's shoulder to cry on," he said, trying to reinforce his case. "But I failed him, too."

"When was that?"

"In my last year at Texas A&M. One of my roommates, Kevin Baker, fell apart when his fiancée, an old high school sweetheart, gave him a Dear John phone call. She'd met another guy at the university she attended. Kevin was heartbroken and started drinking heavily and ditching class. I tried to be supportive but couldn't seem to get through to him. So I avoided going home to the apartment we shared."

"And you think you failed him, too?" she asked.

"Fortunately, another roommate stepped up to the plate, insisting Kevin seek help through the counseling services at school—much to my relief."

"Just because—"

"No, you don't understand. I don't deal well with tears and sorrow. And when things get emotionally heavy, I run in the opposite direction."

"Maybe you sensed your other buddy would step in and Kevin would connect better with him."

Cowboy chuffed. "All I know is that I failed to reach him. And when my granddad had a stroke two weeks later, I used it as an excuse to quit college and cut all ties with my roommates—both of them."

His family hadn't been pleased about his decision, but they'd learned it was fruitless to argue with a natural-born rebel.

And hopefully Prissy would see that, too.

Priscilla placed a kiss on Cowboy's brow. Couldn't he see that guilt and sympathy were emotions, too? And that not talking about what he was feeling didn't make them go away?

He might be afraid to tap into his heart, but he had one. A good one.

She'd seen him reach out to Tyler, a fatherless child, when he'd offered to take him on that outing at the lake—no questions asked.

And he'd been there for her time and again, offering her a hand to hold or a shoulder to lean on. Didn't he see how supportive he really was?

She suspected Cowboy's upbringing had contributed to him feeling inadequate when it came to emotional issues.

"How about your mom?" she asked. "Did she ever apologize to you for being so rude to Jenny?"

"Yeah. A couple of times, actually. But I've never really forgiven her for it."

"That's too bad."

He shrugged. "There's a lot standing in the way of us having any kind of a normal relationship. She and I were never really close. And ever since

Jenny's death, there's been a cold war going on between us."

"What about your dad?"

"He died when I was nine."

"I'm sorry to hear that." Priscilla wanted to reach out to the little boy and to the lonely teenager Cowboy used to be.

Yet he only brushed away her sympathy. "I've put it all behind me. And I've become a better man because of it."

She hoped that was true.

"You know," he added, "I can't really blame my mother completely for the relationship we have. I used to do some pretty ornery things to get back at her when I was in high school and college."

"What kinds of things?"

"I used to purposely take home women she wouldn't approve of. Friends of mine who put on an act, pretending to be hookers, gold diggers and that sort of thing."

"Just to upset her?"

"Yep. And it used to work. She expects a lot out of the family, especially the in-laws. And the girls tried hard *not* to live up to her prim-and-proper standards."

Cowboy had complained that Priscilla had been too prim and proper. Had he thought she was the woman his family *would* approve of?

He slid his arm out from under her. "Why don't we take a quick shower, then I'll take you back to the B and B so you can change before going to see your family?"

She looked to the floor, where her clothing had been scattered.

What would Hildy think when Priscilla walked into the Posey house looking as though she'd slept in her clothes?

Cowboy headed for the bathroom, the back of his hair having an after-the-loving look.

She couldn't help but admire his naked form, his broad shoulders and narrow hips.

"Hey," she said, catching his attention and causing him to turn and flash her the nicest of his features—and she wasn't just talking about his gorgeous eyes and that endearing grin.

"What?" he asked.

"Would your mother approve of me?"

"Yep." He nodded. "No doubt about it. But don't get any ideas. I'm not ready to settle down."

No, he probably wasn't ready yet.

But someday he would be.

And Priscilla planned to be the woman he was with when that happened.

Chapter Twelve

Cowboy sat at the desk in his motel room while Prissy took a morning shower.

He still had reservations about getting involved with her, but the sex had been great, and his attraction to her had only grown stronger. So it just sort of...happened.

The morning after they'd slept together the first time, while she was at the B and B changing her clothes, Cowboy had gone to the drugstore and purchased a box of condoms.

When he came back to pick her up, he learned that she planned to keep her room at the Posey house, which was just as well. The fact that she had a place of her own made it seem as though they weren't really…together. Or whatever it was.

Of course, it didn't take him long to figure out that Prissy's reason for maintaining separate rooms was because she was still on a what-will-people-think? kick, which was silly, if you asked him.

Prissy hadn't slept in her bed for a couple of nights now, and Hildy had to have figured that out. And she probably suspected that Prissy and Cowboy had been tearing up the sheets and steaming up the windows at the Stardust Inn—which is exactly what they'd been doing.

It seemed hard to believe that great sex could improve, but each time they came together was better than the last.

Fortunately they hadn't talked about where their relationship was going—which was good, because if she backed him into a corner, he'd have to bail out. And he wasn't ready to do that yet.

If truth be told, he enjoyed having Prissy's smile be the last thing he saw before closing his eyes at night and the first thing he woke to in the morning.

So for now, he was okay with things just the way they were.

This morning, while he waited for Prissy to take a shower, he looked over the fax he'd received from the Boise chamber of commerce last night. He'd requested a list of local construction companies, and this morning he'd started contacting everyone on the list.

After eight phone calls, he'd been able to scratch several companies, since none of the owners knew Frank Markham. He'd reached an answering machine at two of them, so he'd left voice-mail messages.

But just minutes ago a man by the name of Sam Eggleston had returned his call, and the case of the missing Frank Markham had been solved. Now all Cowboy had to do was head over to the Lone Oak and tell Becky. And then she could figure out how to tell Tyler his father was never coming back.

As the blow-dryer in the bathroom shut off, Cowboy took a sip of the coffee he'd made from the little packets and the four-serving pot in the room. It had tasted like crap when it had been hot, and now that it was room temperature…

He glanced at his watch. It was just after ten o'clock, and he was getting hungry.

Frankly, he was getting a little tired of the food at the Lone Oak, although he was growing fond of the people.

And that was a scary thought for a guy who'd always been on the edge of things.

As the bathroom door swung open, Prissy walked out wearing the pair of cropped black pants and the snug lime-green tank top she'd bought on a shopping spree with her mom and sister yesterday.

Damn, she looked good dressed like that.

She blessed him with a pretty smile, then strode to the desk where he was sitting.

He moved the chair back, making room for her

on his lap, where she sat, wrapped her arms around him and gave him a long, blood-stirring kiss.

No doubt about it. Prissy had begun to let her hair down, and he was liking it.

A lot.

The kiss ended, but he continued to hold her and soak up the peachy scent of her new shampoo, the citrus fragrance of the body lotion she'd picked up in town.

"Are you hungry?" she asked.

"For you. But I guess that will have to wait. We need to go over to the Lone Oak."

"All right," she said. "What's up?"

"I got word on Frank Markham."

"Is he…?"

"Yeah," Cowboy said. "He's dead. But hopefully the fact that he didn't purposely desert Tyler will be of some consolation."

She climbed from his lap, and he picked up the car keys from the table. Then they headed to the bar.

When they arrived, Becky, Harley and Tyler were eating sausage-and-egg burritos at one of the center tables. He assumed Kayla Rae was working with the vet today.

"Can I get you kids something to eat?" Becky asked.

Cowboy glanced at Tyler, then at Becky. "Sure, if you don't mind."

Prissy followed her mom into the kitchen, where Cowboy assumed she would help Becky prepare a couple more burritos.

"You two were a hoot last night," Harley said. "Best laugh I'd had in ages."

Cowboy shot him a crooked grin. "Yeah. We had a lot of fun."

"And correct me if I'm wrong," Harley added, "but you never had anything stronger to drink than soda pop."

He was right. There hadn't been any need. He and Prissy had danced the night away, and a couple of diet colas had done the trick.

"If I hadn't been mixing drinks and filling your glasses myself, I would have thought Priscilla had been drunker than a cross-eyed skunk when she challenged Thelma and Earl to a game of darts. They're the resident champs."

Cowboy laughed. He and Prissy had gotten their butts whipped, but he'd had more fun last night than he could remember.

Imagine that.

"Priscilla may live in the city," Cowboy said, "but apparently she's a down-home country girl at heart."

Harley nodded as he popped the last of his burrito into his mouth. Then he reached for his fork and snagged a chunk of egg that had fallen onto his plate.

Apparently, the stoic bartender had started to open up.

Cowboy supposed Harley must be the kind of man who kept to himself until he'd had a chance to size up a stranger.

Moments later Becky brought the plates to the table while Prissy carried two glasses of orange juice.

"Mom says Sweetie Pie's puppies are really getting big," Prissy told Tyler. "I don't suppose you'd mind showing them to me."

"Heck no." The boy quickly slid off his seat. "They're really cute. And if you want to have one, we'll let you have first pick."

"I'm not sure what I'd do with a dog in the city," Prissy said, following his lead, "but I'd love to see them."

When they were out of sight and earshot, Becky took a seat. "Priscilla said you have news about Frank."

Her expression implied that she knew he was dead but wanted to hear the details.

"I talked to Sam Eggleston," Cowboy said. "He's the old friend who'd offered Frank a job. Apparently Frank arrived safely in Boise and put in a full week at work. Then on payday, he went to a seedy bar in a neighboring town."

"Why doesn't that surprise me?" Becky asked. "Frank just couldn't seem to stay home and out of trouble in the evenings."

"It's not clear exactly what happened, since no one has been charged, but Frank was beat over the head in the parking lot and robbed. A customer found him unconscious and lying in a pool of blood. They called the paramedics and he was rushed to the hospital. But he never came to. He died the next day."

Becky blew out a heavy sigh. "I had a feeling something like that must have happened."

"Sam knew Frank had a son but had no idea who was taking care of him. If you don't mind me giving him your address, he'd like to send you Frank's personal effects and a check for Tyler." Cowboy shrugged. "He said it's not much but that Frank was an old friend and it's the least he can do."

Becky placed a hand on Cowboy's arm. "Thanks for getting to the bottom of this for me. I had no idea where to start."

Cowboy nodded. "Tyler needs to be told."

"Yes, I know." Becky removed her hand from his arm and brushed a strand of hair from her cheek. "In his heart I think he realizes something bad must have happened to his father. I'm sure the truth will hurt, but it's better than not knowing anything."

Cowboy agreed.

Becky blew out a sigh, then clucked her tongue. She glanced at Cowboy, then at Harley. "What is it about men? Why can't they stay out of trouble and put their kids and their families first?"

"You can't judge all men by the couple of rascals you've had to deal with," Harley said.

"It's hard not to," Becky said.

Cowboy could understand why she'd feel that way.

"Don't let anger and an unforgiving spirit eat away at you." Harley placed his hand on top of Becky's. "And it will if you let it."

"You're probably right. But what Cliff did to me

was unforgivable," Becky said. "And it's made me leery about getting involved with another man again."

"I've been hurt in the past, too," Harley told her. "But anger and resentment are self-destructive."

The truth of Harley's words settled around Cowboy. The man was probably right.

Thank God Cowboy had learned how to skate around his anger and resentment years ago. And there was nothing self-destructive about that.

Priscilla sat on the side of the tub in her mother's mobile home and studied the six squirming puppies. They were darling, especially the runt, a black-and-white spotted male.

"Want to hold one?" Tyler asked.

"Sure. How about the little guy?"

He reached for the runt, then handed it to her.

"Hey, there." She placed the puppy against her cheek, marveling at his soft fur, his warm body, his sweet face. "You're a little love."

"He probably won't get too big," Tyler said. "Maybe you can sneak him on the airplane when you go back home."

"He'll be too young to go with me this time." Priscilla planned to fly back to New York this weekend and return to work on Monday.

And even though she looked forward to seeing Sylvia and getting back to the city, she wasn't in a hurry to leave Cotton Creek.

What was with that?

The bond she was developing with her family, she supposed. But she suspected it might be her relationship with Cowboy, too. What they had in Cotton Creek was special. Would things change in New York?

Probably.

She handed the runt back to Tyler, who placed him near his mother.

"Come on," she told the boy. "Let's go back and see the others."

Hopefully Cowboy had been able to reveal what had happened to Frank by now.

When they returned to the bar, Becky stood, then took Tyler by the hand and walked him outside.

Priscilla suspected her mother was going to tell him what had happened to his father, and her heart went out to the little boy.

When Harley excused himself to go into the storeroom, she and Cowboy were left alone.

"Poor kid." Cowboy's sympathy for the child touched her. He might be uncomfortable dealing with his feelings, but he obviously had them.

And since he had lost his own father as a child, he knew what Tyler was going through. It would sure be nice if he would share his loss with the boy.

Of course, after he'd admitted his struggle to offer emotional support, she couldn't very well spring the suggestion on him. So, hoping he'd take the hint and make the suggestion himself, she quizzed him about his relationship with his father.

"Were you close to your dad?" she asked.

"As close as I was to anyone, I suppose."

"It must have been tough to lose him at such a young age."

He shrugged. "My dad was a workaholic, so I didn't get to spend much time with him."

"That's too bad."

"Yeah, it was. And it was a shock, too. One night, while he was working late at the office, he had a heart attack." Cowboy paused.

Reflecting, she supposed.

"You know," he said, "I've always wondered if my dad could have been saved if someone else had been in the building that night—or if he'd been at home, where he belonged."

"His death must have been tough, especially on all of you kids."

"I guess it was. My brothers and sisters felt bad and cried at the funeral, but I don't think they missed him all that much. And neither did my mom, who'd been keeping herself busy with philanthropic endeavors after the older kids went off to college and left home."

"I'm sorry," she said again.

He seemed to shrug off her sympathy.

"Maybe since you went through the same thing, it would help if you talked to Tyler."

"No way," Cowboy said. "I'm not going to risk screwing up something like that."

She'd seen Cowboy with Tyler and she knew how supportive he'd been with her. So she had no doubt that he'd say the right thing, even if he was afraid he wouldn't. But before she could contemplate a response, his cell phone rang.

Just in the nick of time, Cowboy thought as he reached for his cell.

The only trouble was, when he looked at the display, he realized it was a call from his mother.

"Hello."

"I hadn't heard from you recently, TJ, and I wanted to remind you about the dinner party I'm hosting on Friday night to kick off Dan's campaign."

He wasn't sure why she'd expected him to call and confirm. He'd told her he'd be there. "I'm flying into Dallas in the afternoon."

"Good," she said. "And by the way, Dan thought you could join him for golf on Saturday."

"Sure. Tell him to get a tee time."

His mother paused as though she had something else on her mind. "Katie will be glad to hear you'll be at the dinner. It's very important to her. And to Dan."

"That's why I agreed to be there."

"I'm not sure what time your flight is," his mother said, "but can you please try to be at the house by five?"

"I thought the wingding didn't start until seven."

"Yes, but Dan's campaign manager wants to prep us beforehand."

As long as traffic wasn't anything out of the

ordinary, he could make it. "I'll see what I can do. I'd planned to check into the hotel, get dressed, then drive out to the house."

"That's not necessary," his mother said. "You can stay here with me."

He glanced at Prissy, wondering how she'd feel about going with him to Dallas, but figuring it was best to take a break from her. Or rather, a break from *them*. Things were going a little too well for his comfort.

"And one more thing," his mother added. "I hope you're not planning on bringing a date."

Actually, the thought had briefly crossed his mind and he'd decided against it. But the fact that his mother had told him not to made the idea all the more appealing. And the rebel in him decided to stir things up for old times' sake. "Why not?"

"I shouldn't have to explain that to you."

He glanced at Prissy, saw her watching him.

She'd asked what his family would think of her, and he'd told her the truth. She'd fit right in.

"I'll see you on Friday," he said. But he just couldn't help setting off his mother one more time. "And if I can rustle up a date, I will bring her along."

"Tren-ton," his mother began, drawing out each syllable of his name in exasperation.

"Not to worry. I'll see you at five on Friday."

His mother was still sputtering when he said goodbye, and he couldn't help but smile.

Normally, he wouldn't take a date to a function

like that, an event that was important to his sister, Katie, and her husband, Dan.

And even though he hadn't pulled any of those tacky-chick pranks on his mother in years, it irked him to know she didn't trust him to behave. Or to be considerate of his sister and her husband.

"Is everything okay?" Prissy asked.

"Just the same old, same old," he admitted.

Did he dare ask Prissy to go with him?

Showing up with her on his arm would unsettle his mother at first—until she got a chance to talk to Prissy and realize she was different from what she'd expected.

Then everything would be all right.

Aw, what the hell.

He reached out and gently tugged on one of Prissy's curls. "If you don't have anything better to do this weekend and you don't mind attending political fund-raisers, maybe you'd like to go with me to Dallas."

Prissy brightened. "Actually, it sounds interesting. I can fly home from Dallas on Sunday rather than San Antonio."

"Good. It's a date."

She flashed him a smile, then began to fret. "I'll have to go shopping. I don't have anything suitable to wear."

"Don't worry. Maybe on the way to the airport in San Antonio we can find a dress shop."

Prissy slid her arms around him and pressed a kiss on his cheek. "You're so sweet. And thoughtful."

No, he wasn't. And now that he'd invited her, a sense of uneasiness washed over him.

Why had he done it? Was it because he wanted to take Prissy home to meet his family and show her off?

Or had he wanted her to see the Whittakers for what they really were?

Maybe a little of both.

But something told him there was another motivating factor, one that had colored a lot of his decisions over the years when it came to his family.

Cowboy had a rebellious streak that just wouldn't die.

On the flight to Dallas Prissy had quizzed Cowboy about his family, about the people she was going to meet. To be honest, she was excited but nervous.

"Don't stress about it," he'd told her. "If anyone ought to be concerned about making a good impression, it should be them."

She glanced down at the new hip-hugging jeans he'd encouraged her to buy while they'd been shopping in San Antonio this morning. He'd thought they'd be more comfortable for traveling and he was probably right.

But he also liked the way her belly button showed when she lifted her arm, which was something she'd have to watch out for.

Their flight had arrived nearly an hour late, so rather than check into the hotel, which was clear across town, they took a cab straight to the house. Cowboy insisted it wouldn't be a problem if they dressed for the dinner at his mother's.

"Tell me about your family," she said, hoping she could keep everyone straight.

"Besides my sister Katie and her husband Dan, my three brothers will be there, too. Ken is the oldest, and he's married to Rita. Bob's wife is Sharon. And Ryan was divorced a while back. I'm not sure if he's seeing anyone." He reached across the seat and took her hand in his. "Seriously, honey, you'll fit right in. Just be yourself and relax."

Yeah. Right. The people she was about to meet could become her future in-laws someday if things eventually worked out the way she hoped they would.

"And they're all involved in the family business?" she asked.

"Yep."

She looked out the window of the cab, watching the scenery, when she realized something.

"Why are you working for Garcia and Associates in New York?"

"I was at Whittaker Enterprises for a while."

"Doing what?"

"Conducting preemployment screenings and background checks. But I didn't like working with my family. And eight years ago, after a run-in with my older brother about the social responsibilities and public appearances associated with being a Whittaker, I got tired of the pretenses and quit."

"Is that when you ended up working for Garcia and Associates?"

"Yep. I started as Rico's assistant but caught on quickly and became a P.I. myself."

As the cabbie pulled into the driveway, he stopped at a security gate.

Cowboy rolled down his window and spoke to the guard. "Trenton Whittaker. We're on the list."

"Yes, sir." The uniformed man checked the paperwork in front of him, then hit a lever that opened the wrought-iron gate.

"Whittaker Enterprises must be some company," Priscilla said.

"It's actually a subsidiary of Whittaker Oil."

"Oh." Wow. She'd had no idea how wealthy Cowboy's family was. They could probably put the Van Zandts to shame.

She looked down at her jeans, at the white blouse that had gotten wrinkled on the plane. Even though she'd loosened up recently, thanks to the influence of her mom and sister, she would have been a lot more comfortable in her cream-colored suit.

As the cab pulled in front of what could only be described as a redbrick mansion, Priscilla was taken aback by the grandeur.

"I feel out of place," she said as Cowboy opened the door. "And underdressed."

He reached for her hand and drew her across the seat. "You look fine, Prissy. They're going to love you. Like I said, all you have to do is be yourself."

That was a lot easier said than done.

Cowboy paid the cabbie, then handed Priscilla the Neiman Marcus bag that protected her new dress on its hanger. Then he grabbed her carry-on and his snazzy garment bag and took them to the front door. He rang the buzzer but didn't wait for anyone to answer.

Once he'd let them inside, Priscilla stepped into the marble-tiled foyer and surveyed the house Cowboy had grown up in. Sylvia's home couldn't even come close to comparing to this.

"TJ," a woman's voice called out from upstairs. "Is that you?"

"Yes," he said. "It's me. What'd you do, run off all the household help?"

"No, I've got them all working on the back patio. The caterer was late."

As Cowboy's mother swept down a circular stairway dressed in a tailored pink Chanel suit, Cowboy said, "Mother, I'd like you to meet Priscilla…Richards."

"Epperson," Priscilla corrected. They hadn't discussed it yet, but she planned to use her real name from now on.

Virginia Whittaker, whose blond hair was coifed to perfection, cast a polite but snooty smile on Priscilla. Then she perused her son and clicked her tongue. "You're not dressed."

"Our flight was late," he explained. "We didn't have time to go to the hotel, but we have our bags. So if you don't mind, we'll get ready here."

Priscilla had felt nervous before, but Mrs. Whittaker's icy demeanor sent her uneasiness into overdrive.

"Why don't you show us where you'd like us to change?" Cowboy asked.

"Very well." As she led them into a living room decorated in shades of cream and beige, she turned to Priscilla. "Where did the two of you meet?"

"In New York," she said, not wanting to go into the details of how and why she'd hired him.

"Is that where your people are from?" she asked.

"I live in Brooklyn, but I was born in Cotton Creek, Texas. That's where my family lives."

"What does your father do?"

"He's deceased," she told her. "But my mother owns and operates the Lone Oak Bar."

"I see," Mrs. Whittaker said.

Maybe Priscilla should have held back that piece of information, but Cowboy had told her to be herself. And quite frankly she was proud of her mother, proud of what she'd done with her life after having suffered so many tragedies.

Mrs. Whittaker pointed out the bathroom.

"You go ahead," Cowboy told her. "I'll use my old bedroom and meet you in the living room."

Priscilla nodded, then took her garment bag and carry-on from him and stepped into one of the fanciest restrooms she'd ever seen, with marble countertops and gold fixtures.

What in the world had she gotten herself into?

* * *

After dressing in the suit he'd brought from Manhattan, Cowboy splashed on a hint of aftershave then headed out to the living room to wait for Prissy.

No one else had arrived yet, but his mother sat on the edge of the sofa, her hands folded and resting in her lap.

"You couldn't help but defy me, could you?" she asked.

"Relax. You're in for a pleasant surprise."

"Am I?" she asked. "How could you do that to your sister? Or to Dan? Why, they've been good to you."

Yeah, they had been. And he wouldn't have done anything to embarrass them. They were going to love Prissy, in spite of his mother's first impression.

He figured that she was fuming about the fact that Prissy's mother owned and managed a bar, but he also assumed she wasn't too impressed by Cotton Creek or Brooklyn.

"So in spite of my wishes, you were compelled to drag home another woman you knew the family wouldn't approve of. Where do you find these people?"

Cowboy wanted to lash out at her, to defend Prissy and their relationship—whatever it had become. But he also struggled to keep his feelings, his vulnerability, to himself. After all, he'd never been good enough, never really been accepted by the family conglomerate.

He opened his mouth, planning to tell his mother that Priscilla wasn't like the other women he'd brought home in an act of rebellion, that she wasn't some floozy he'd met in a bar. She was cultured, educated, sophisticated. That she might even be the kind of woman he could…fall in love with someday.

But his mom would only scoff and turn up her nose. So he played the old game and shrugged off the accusation.

Until he heard someone clear her throat from the doorway.

They both turned to see Prissy, wearing her pretty new dress and her hair styled to perfection.

It was enough to make him beam with pride—if the pain in her expression hadn't ripped open his chest.

Chapter Thirteen

Priscilla didn't know what hurt worse—Virginia Whittaker's criticism or Cowboy's lack of support.

But it wasn't just his failure to defend her that stung. It was his betrayal.

He'd told her about taking home dates his mother wouldn't approve of in the past. And apparently he'd done it again. He'd used her to get back at someone else—just as her father had used her to get back at her mother all those years ago.

Tears sprang to her eyes, and her heart threatened to burst from her chest.

But she was determined not to make a scene. So

she turned to Cowboy's mother. "Do you mind if I use your phone, Mrs. Whittaker?"

"No. It's in the study." The elegantly dressed woman pointed a manicured finger toward a set of double doors on the left.

"Who are you calling?" Cowboy asked.

"It's personal." She fingered the shoulder strap of her black purse, then strode toward the den.

Once inside, she closed the door and picked up the phone. Then she dialed information and asked for the number of a local cab company. When she had someone on the line, it took her a moment to recall the address.

Closing her eyes, she tried to picture the block pillar they'd passed as they'd entered the estate.

1492 Peachtree Lane.

The dispatcher told her it would be about twenty minutes, which she supposed wasn't anything to complain about. She would just walk down to the security gate and wait.

She certainly didn't want to stay in this house a minute longer. And the sooner she could escape—

Thoughts of her father came barreling down on her, stopping her in her tracks. The memory of the night he'd sneaked into the Posey house and kidnapped her blazed like a flashing red light. That was the night Clifford Epperson had run away from his troubles.

And here she was, poised on the brink of doing the very same thing.

But running wasn't going to solve anything.

She loved her father and always would, but she saw him for what he was—weak and a coward.

Just as quickly as her father's memory came into play, so did an image of her mother, a single woman who'd faced her problems head-on.

What would Rebecca Posey Epperson do in a situation like this?

She'd been crushed when her daughter had been kidnapped, but she'd trudged on. And when Kayla Rae had needed open-heart surgery soon after birth, Becky had tapped into her inner strength. Then, when facing a mountain of debt, she'd sold the family house and gone to work to make a living and provide a home for herself and her daughters—the one she was able to rock to sleep and the one she hoped would someday return to her arms.

No. Becky wouldn't run off with her tail between her legs. If she were in this position, she'd march right back into the living room with her head held high.

And that was exactly what Priscilla would do.

At one time she'd thought she needed someone to lean on, but not anymore. She'd just have to rely on herself, as she'd always done. But from now on she would be more proactive when it came to her life and her future.

And she didn't give a damn what anyone thought.

She strode out of the den and into the living room.

Cowboy stood when she entered and made his way toward her. "I need to talk to you." Then he took her by the hand, led her back into the study and closed the door. "I don't know how much you heard."

"Enough to know you had a reason for buying me those low-riding jeans. And it wasn't because I have a cute belly button."

"That's not true." He slid her the crooked grin she'd always found endearing. "You've got an adorable belly button."

"Don't try to lay the charm on me," she told him. "It won't work."

His expression sobered, and regret peered through his eyes. "Honey, you might not believe this, but I care for you. *A lot.* And I'm looking forward to introducing you to my family and friends. We'll make it a short evening. Or if you'd rather leave now, I'll take you wherever you want to go."

"Don't bother changing your plans for me. I've called a cab, so I don't need you to take me anywhere. I'll just say what needed to be said moments ago. And then I'm going home."

He reached for her hand. "The only reason I didn't say squat to my mother is because there's never been any use putting my best foot forward. She's never been happy with me, so it didn't matter anyway."

She withdrew her hand from his grip, severing the connection. "Cowboy, you're an emotional coward, and until you're honest about what you're feeling and get the nerve to stumble and fumble through your emotions like the rest of us do on a daily basis, you're going to be a very unhappy man."

Then she returned to the living room, where Her Royal Highness sat primly on the edge of a brocade sofa, hands clasped lightly in her lap.

"I apologize for what I said," Virginia Whittaker said coolly. "I hadn't realized you were within hearing distance."

"My instinct tells me you're only sorry that I overheard your comment, but I'll accept your apology anyway and put this all behind me."

How could she do anything else? Even as she stood there, chin held high, her heart was breaking, her dreams dissipating.

Cowboy took her hand again and brushed his thumb across her wrist. She suspected he felt the steady beat of her pulse. She felt it, too, pounding with the strength she'd inherited from her mother.

"Listen, Prissy—"

"No, *you* listen. *Both of you.*" Her eyes flitted from Cowboy, who appeared shaken, to his mother, who seemed taken aback. "I might not have the kind of background the Whittaker family would be proud of, but I've got the strength of my mother flowing in my veins. A woman I've grown to admire and love."

Cowboy slipped an arm around her waist. "I'm sorry my mom jumped to conclusions, honey. But as soon as she spends five minutes with you, she'll realize how wrong she was."

"Don't worry about what was said. I'm proud of

who I am and where I'm from, and a few snobby words from someone with very little *real* class aren't going to cause me to lose sleep. But you, on the other hand, betrayed me by bringing me here and setting me up."

Mrs. Whittaker released a little gasp, but she didn't respond.

"I didn't invite you to come here as a prank," Cowboy said. "And when my mother spouted off, I should have spoken up."

"But you didn't."

Cowboy merely stood there, watching the woman he'd also misjudged.

Prissy had always worried about what other people thought of her and she'd wanted so badly to fit in, to be accepted by his family. But when push came to shove, she was standing tall and showing her mettle.

And he respected her for it.

But she was turning her back on him, on what they'd shared.

Other than continue to apologize, which wasn't his style, he couldn't think of anything else to do or say that would change her mind, make her understand.

She'd called him an emotional coward. And as bad as that sounded, it was true.

He could snap at his mother, he supposed, as he'd done a hundred times before. But somehow he didn't think that was going to do the trick.

Prissy had been getting at something else. Something deeper. Something that would make him more vulnerable than he'd been for a long time.

But it would take courage to open his guts for the first time in years. To tell his mother that ever since he was a child, all he'd ever wanted was her love and acceptance. To admit that he'd only rebelled as a means of self-protection.

No, he couldn't do that. Not here. Not now. Not when Dan's political gathering was about to begin.

And maybe not ever.

The last time he'd opened up his heart to his mom, he'd been Tyler's age. He'd been hurting and missing his dad something awful. And he'd wanted her to hold him, to tell him everything would be okay. But instead she'd brushed a kiss across his brow and passed him off to the nanny. Then she'd hurried off to some damned fund-raiser that supported disadvantaged kids.

Her rejection had hurt, but his pain had slowly turned to resentment. He'd buried his feelings for years, but it all came back now, and the wound was just as raw as it had ever been.

The doorbell sounded, and his sister's voice sounded in the foyer. "Mother! We're here."

Dan and Katie entered the living room with a silver-haired gentleman Cowboy didn't recognize. Dan introduced him as Stanley Peters, the campaign manager. And Katie gave her little brother a quick welcome-home hug.

When the greetings were over, Cowboy again slipped an arm around Prissy's waist and drew her close. "I'd like you to meet Priscilla Epperson, a good friend of mine."

At least, they'd been friends before.

They'd been lovers, too.

Was that all going to change? Before he was ready for it to?

He'd let Prissy down, just as he'd let Jenny down years ago. And he didn't blame her for being hurt, angry.

Was there anything he could do to repair the damage he'd done?

Priscilla reached out a hand in greeting, her cool demeanor immediately lifting for Katie and Dan.

"It's nice to meet you," Katie said as she took Prissy's hand. "What a lovely dress. It looks great on you. I saw one like it at Neiman Marcus and I nearly bought it. But it wouldn't have looked nearly as nice on me."

Then Katie turned to Cowboy. "I'm so glad you decided to bring a date. Dan's campaign focuses on family values, and it makes you look a lot more settled than you were in those wild and woolly days."

For the first time in his life Cowboy found it hard to respond.

What would his sister say when Prissy hightailed it out of here in a cab?

And worse, what was he going to do when she left?

Again, the doorbell rang, and as the rest of the

Whittaker clan arrived in a steady stream, the introductions quickly continued.

"Now that you're all here," Dan said, "Stanley wants to go over a few things."

The family matriarch swept her arm toward the study. "Let's retire to somewhere more private."

As they all headed toward the double doors, Prissy tugged at Cowboy's sleeve. "Do you have your cell phone handy?"

"Yep. Why?"

"I'd like you to call the Yellow Rose Cab Company and cancel my request—*for now.*"

Whether it was Katie's warm acceptance or the mention of family values that caused Prissy to decide to stick it out this evening didn't matter.

"I'd be happy to make that call," he said. "You go inside with the others and I'll join you in a minute."

Then, as he headed down the hall to place the call in his old bedroom, he blew out a sigh of relief.

This might be the calm before the storm, but at least he had one last chance to make things right.

Because until Prissy blessed him with another smile, his whole world was on edge.

As the evening progressed, everything fell into place.

Cowboy's mother easily slipped into superhostess mode and worked the party as only she knew how, while Prissy carried herself with grace and style, chatting with the other guests.

There wasn't even a hint of the tension that had filled the room just an hour earlier.

But Cowboy, who was trying his best to go through the glad-you-came, it's-good-to-see-you-again motions, hadn't been able to put the confrontation with Prissy behind him. He couldn't forget her words, her accusation. Nor could he disregard the truth.

Things might appear picture-perfect on the surface, but until Cowboy could get Prissy alone, until he could make things right between them, he was still uneasy.

In fact, he couldn't tear his eyes away from her all evening while he watched her mingle with the crowd, saying all the right things, charming all the right people—a trick that had always been his forte. But she'd thrown him off balance earlier, and he found it difficult to be his carefree, easygoing self.

During the cocktail hour, Prissy had seemed to hit it off with everyone she met. As the campaign manager had advised earlier, she skated around talk of politics like a pro, which in this crowd was an art in and of itself, even if she had graduated from Brown and hobnobbed with the Van Zandts. She also managed to have some interesting conversations along the way. She spoke to Conrad Hunter about several Broadway plays they'd both seen. And after talking to Caroline Burch for a few minutes, they found a shared interest in English literature and Elizabethan history.

During dinner she sat next to Vince Bishop, a fifty-something business exec who admitted to having a story inside of him and asking her for tips on how to find a ghostwriter.

All in all, the event went well, even though Cowboy had endured the evening with a phony grin.

Before long, checks had been written or promised, and the crowd began to disperse.

Katie and Dan went outdoors to see their supporters off, and Cowboy followed them. He was eager to send everyone on their way and get some time alone with Prissy. He had to make her see how sorry he was, had to keep her from leaving.

Earlier, he'd suspected his feelings for her were growing serious. But he was more sure now.

When she'd first started to whittle away at his hardened heart, he'd been afraid of getting in too deep and failing her, as he had Jenny.

But Prissy wasn't anything like the fragile teenager he'd once dated, a troubled young girl who'd buckled under pressure from his mother. And she wasn't like Cowboy, either.

She faced her feelings and her problems rather than dodging them.

Even after suffering an emotional blow and learning of her father's deceit, she'd coped, confronted her past and moved on with her life.

And it was time for him to do the same thing.

When Prissy walked out with Rhonda Bainbridge, he figured it was the perfect time to get her aside, to take her for a walk in the garden and settle things between them. Maybe if he played his cards right, if he could convince her he was determined to open his heart, he'd steal a kiss or two until they could get back to the hotel and forget this mess by making love until dawn.

"There he is," Rhonda said, pointing to a black limousine that pulled into the circular drive and slowed to a stop. "That's our car and driver."

"I'll get my bag," Prissy said.

Her bag?

Cowboy drew Prissy aside. "Where do you think you're going?"

"Rhonda and Phillip are going to drop me off at the airport."

The reality of her decision struck a hard blow, threatening to shatter his already vulnerable heart. "You changed your ticket already?"

"I plan to do that at the airport. And if I can't get a flight out tonight, I'll get a hotel room and fly out in the morning."

"You need to wait—please—just a little while longer. And if you want to be dropped off at the airport later tonight or at a different hotel, I'll take you."

She paused for the longest time, and it seemed as though his future hung in the balance.

Emotion brewed under his skin, something strong and compelling. Something that told him his life would be empty without Prissy at his side.

"All right," she said. "I'll wait."

"Good." He reached for her hand. "Come with me."

He led her back into the house, where he found his mother in the living room.

Alone.

His urge was to turn around, to walk out without looking back. But he had to get something off his chest, something that had been rooted in his heart and would shadow his love for Priscilla.

"We need to talk, Mother."

The Whittaker matriarch turned, and suddenly he felt like a kid again. A nine-year-old child who desperately needed the reassurance of a mother's love.

"You're right. There are things that need to be said." Her gaze drifted to Prissy. "I want you to know I was wrong about you, dear. My comment was rude and uncalled for." Then she looked at Cowboy. "And you were right, son. It didn't take long for me to realize Priscilla isn't at all like the other women you brought home. She carries herself very well."

"I'm glad you've come to that conclusion," he said, "but that's not what I wanted to discuss."

"Then what's on your mind, Trenton?"

He led Priscilla to the sofa, where they both took a seat. "I want to start by having a heart-to-heart conversation with you, Mom. Something that should have been done a long time ago."

She merely sat there, watching. Waiting.

"I apologize for being so rebellious in the past."

The brow over her left eye twitched, suggesting

she was as surprised as he was at the way things were unfolding.

"I've always felt as though my best was never good enough, so back when I was still a kid, I quit trying to vie for your attention, opting to get your goat instead."

"You certainly were a master at that," she said, her lips quirking into an ever-so-slight smile.

"I want to bury the hatchet and end that cold war we've been having for years."

His mother nodded. "I'm ready to call a truce, too."

Then he turned to Prissy. "I haven't said this to anyone since I was nine years old. And I swore I never would again. But I love you, Priscilla."

A tear slipped down her cheek, then another. But instead of wanting to run in the opposite direction, he wanted to hold her close, to offer whatever he could, whatever he had.

"And if you'll have me," he added, "I want to marry you."

She swiped at her eyes and smiled. "I love you, too."

Her words shot straight to his heart, flooding his chest with warmth and making him vow to be the kind of man she deserved.

He wrapped her in his arms and gave her a long, lingering kiss, a kiss that promised he'd do his best to never fail her.

As her lips parted, he savored her sweet taste and

relished her soft floral scent, basking in the realization that in her embrace he'd found the love he'd been missing, a love that would last forever.

His mother cleared her throat, reminding them where they were.

When they came up for air, his smiling mom reached out a hand to Priscilla. "I suppose it's only right that I welcome my future daughter-in-law into the fold. I always knew it would take a strong woman to tame Trenton. And I can see you're the one to do it."

As the women's fingers wrapped around each other, the cold war officially ended.

"Come on, honey," Cowboy said as he stood and took Priscilla's hand. "Let's go home."

Of course, all they had to do was figure out exactly where that would be—his loft or a new place of their own.

But whether they were in New York or visiting in Texas, home would always be wherever Prissy was.

Cowboy had suggested Rico's wife, who was a bridal consultant, plan the wedding, but Molly had just found out she was pregnant with twins and was suffering from morning sickness. Since Rico insisted she stick close to home, another consultant was chosen.

There would be nearly four hundred people in attendance. So it seemed only natural for Priscilla to have three bridal showers—one hosted by Sylvia in Manhattan, another that Katie would have at her home in Dallas next week, and this one that Kayla Rae was throwing today in Cotton Creek.

The Lone Oak Bar had been decorated for the occasion. The walls and ceilings were adorned with crepe-paper swirls and the scarred tabletops were hidden by pastel-colored tablecloths, white votive candles and bouquets of flowers in mason jars.

Priscilla sat at the center table with her future in-laws: Virginia, Katie, Rita and Sharon. Her mom and Kayla Rae, who were busy making sure everything was going smoothly, would also be seated with them.

"This is such a fun location for a shower," Katie said as she scanned the room. Then she looked at her mother. "Don't you agree?"

"Well," Virginia said, "I have to admit, I've never been in a place like this before, let alone imagined it as a setting for a bridal shower. But it's…unique."

Priscilla had to give Cowboy's mother credit for trying to blend into a world that was completely foreign to her. But ever since the mother and son had entered into a closer, more honest relationship, things had been much better. And they were both trying hard to be considerate of each other and their feelings.

Kayla Rae stopped by the table long enough to tell them it was time to eat and that since they were the guests of honor, they should start the buffet line.

"There are salads and sandwiches," Kayla Rae

added, "and a special batch of my mother's Snake-adillo Chili."

Virginia cleared her throat. "My…uh…stomach sometimes acts up when I travel, so I probably ought to pass on anything…spicy."

Kayla Rae patted her on the wrist. "Now, don't you worry about that. We keep a big supply of antacids behind the bar—just in case."

As they made their way to the buffet, Virginia whispered to Priscilla, "Pray tell. What in the world is in that chili?"

"The typical barnyard variety of meat," Priscilla whispered back. "But don't let anyone else know. It's a big secret. And believe it or not, the chili is worth any antacid chasers you might need to take later."

Virginia cleared her throat. "Will your mother's feelings be hurt if I pass on it anyway?"

"I wouldn't worry about it. My mom is pretty tough." Priscilla glanced across the room, where her mother was handing Tyler a plate of food before shooing him out the back door to eat with Harley.

When Becky looked up, she flashed Priscilla a smile and mouthed, *I love you.*

Priscilla did the same.

"You've been good for Trenton," Virginia said as she picked up a plate and handed another to Priscilla. "I've never seen him so settled, so happy."

"Your son has been good for me, too," Priscilla told her. And not just because of the whopping big diamond ring that now graced her left hand. Love had been instrumental in creating positive changes in them both.

Minutes later, when Priscilla and her future in-laws returned to the table with their plates piled high, her mother joined them, carrying a tray with small bowls.

"Did everyone get a chance to taste the Snake-adillo Chili?" Becky asked.

"I'll try it," Katie said.

Rita laughed. "Why not? I'll have some, too."

"So will I," Sharon said.

"I'll…" Virginia began. "Oh, for goodness sake. Give me one of those, too. But I'm only going to have a little taste."

Becky passed out the bowls, and Katie took the first bite. "Mmm. This is really good."

"Is it?" Rita dug in next. "Ooh. You're right."

"You know," Sharon said, "I don't normally eat chili, Becky, but this is the best I've ever had."

Virginia carefully picked up her spoon, then scooped out a dollop and placed it in her mouth.

"Well, now," she said, "that was…quite good, if you like chili."

She didn't finish her bowl, but at least she'd given it a try.

After lunch, Kayla Rae introduced the only game they would play, calling it Cupid.

On the far wall she hung a life-size picture of a Texas ranger. There was a red circle drawn around the badge on his chest.

"This game is like Pin the Tail on the Donkey with a twist." Kayla held up a bright red dart. "This is Cupid's arrow. Whoever strikes closest to the target will win the prize."

"That's no fair," a woman in back called out. "Thelma is going to win this hands down."

Katie nudged Priscilla. "Who's Thelma?"

"She's the better half of the resident dart champs."

"Don't worry," Kayla Rae told the woman in back. "Thelma is going to have to stand ten feet farther than the rest of you."

Amidst the cheers of the shower guests, Katie took top honors of the game and won a box of stationery and a pen.

Next, while Priscilla opened a mound of gifts, Kayla Rae and Becky passed out pieces of chocolate fudge cake—another of Becky's homemade specialties.

As Priscilla reached for a present, Cowboy entered the bar.

He made his way to Priscilla, then brushed a kiss across her cheek. "Am I too early?"

"No, you're just in time to help me open the last one." She reached for the big box that had been wrapped in pink floral paper and removed the card.

It was from her mother.

Priscilla smiled warmly at her mom, then removed the white bow and carefully opened a box that was large enough to hold luggage.

But inside she found a framed portrait of a young couple holding a baby girl.

The man had dark hair and a handsome smile. The woman had hair the color of Priscilla's.

"Who are they?" she asked.

"It's my mom and dad," Becky said. "And the baby is me."

"And you're giving this to me?"

Her mom's eyes filled with tears. "My parents were very special people, and the good Lord took them home before I was ready to live without them. But whenever I looked at their picture, whenever I remembered how much they loved me, how much they believed in me, I was able to go on. And since you never had the chance to know them, I wanted you to have it."

Tears of gratitude and appreciation gathered in Priscilla's eyes. "I wish I would have known them."

"They would have loved you, honey. Just as much as I do."

Priscilla stood and wrapped her mother in a warm embrace. "I'm so sorry we missed out on the early years together, but we have the rest of our lives to make up for it. I love you, Mom."

"And I love you, honey." When Becky released her, she turned to Cowboy. "And I love you, too, young man. But don't you ever let that little girl down or you'll have to answer to me."

"And to me," Virginia added. "You couldn't have found a better match, TJ."

"I agree." Cowboy took Priscilla into his arms. "I'm the luckiest man in the world."

"And I'm the luckiest woman," Priscilla added.

Then, amidst the cheers of the bridal shower guests, they sealed their love with a kiss.

* * * * *

SPECIAL EDITION™

THE LAST COWBOY

BY

CRYSTAL GREEN

Felicia Markowski wants children
more than anything, but her infertility
is an obstacle she cannot overcome.
But when she meets handsome cowboy
Jackson North—a brooding man with a
past—she wonders if fate has other plans
for her after all.

Look for this story
April 2006.